BOY21

MATTHEW QUICK

headline

First published in Great Britain in 2014 by
HEADLINE PUBLISHING GROUP

1

Cataloguing in Publication Data is available from the British Library

ISBN 978 1 4722 1290 0

Typeset in Granjon by Palimpsest Book Production Limited,
Falkirk, Stirlingshire

Printed and bound in Great Britain by Clays Ltd, St Ives plc

Headline's policy is to use papers that are natural, renewable and recyclable products and
made from wood grown in sustainable forests. The logging and manufacturing processes
are expected to conform to the environmental
regulations of the country of origin.

HEADLINE PUBLISHING GROUP
An Hachette UK Company
338 Euston Road
London NW1 3BH

www.headline.co.uk
www.hachette.co.uk

Matthew Quick (aka Q) is the *New York Times*-bestselling author of several novels, including THE SILVER LININGS PLAYBOOK, which was made into an Academy Award-winning film. His work has been translated into more than twenty languages and has received a PEN/Hemingway Award Honorable Mention, among other accolades. Q lives in Massachusetts with his wife, novelist/pianist Alicia Bessette.

Praise for Matthew Quick:

'Very serious subjects handled with great sensitivity and a high dose of comedy. Brilliant' *Image*

'The most moving novel we've read in a long time . . . Funny and heartbreaking, this will leave a lasting impression' *Bella*

'A raw, devastating and very real offering' *Look*

By Matthew Quick:

THE SILVER LININGS PLAYBOOK
SORTA LIKE A ROCKSTAR
BOY 21
FORGIVE ME, LEONARD PEACOCK
THE GOOD LUCK OF RIGHT NOW

For all my brothers
From different mothers

PREFACE

Sometimes I pretend that shooting hoops in my backyard is my earliest memory.

I'm just a kid, so Dad gives me one of those smaller basketballs and lowers the adjustable rim. He tells me to shoot until I can make one hundred baskets in a row, which seems impossible. Then he goes back inside the house to deal with my pop, who has recently returned legless from the hospital, clutching my dead grandmother's rosary beads. Our house has been silent for a long time and I understand that my mother is not coming back, but I don't want to think about what happened, so I do as my father instructed.

At first, I can't even reach the rim when I shoot, even though the hoop has been lowered. I keep shooting for hours and hours, until my neck is stiff from looking up and I'm sweaty. When the sun goes down, Dad puts on the floodlight and I continue to take shots, because it's better than being inside listening to my pop cry and moan – and, also, it's what Dad told me to do.

In my memory, I shoot through the night and don't stop for days and weeks and months. I don't even break to eat or sleep or use the bathroom. I just keep shooting hoops, zoning out, pretending that I will never have to go into my house again – that I will never have to remember what happened before I began shooting hoops.

You can lose yourself in repetition – quiet your thoughts; I learned the value of this at a very young age.

I remember the leaves falling and crunching under my feet, the snowflakes burning my skin, the yellow long-stem flowers blooming by the fence, and then being scorched by the powerful July sun – through it all I kept shooting.

I must have done other things – like go to school, obviously – but shooting hoops in my backyard is the only thing I remember from childhood.

After a few years, Dad began speaking more and shooting with me, which was nice.

Sometimes, Pop would park his wheelchair at the end of the driveway and sip a beer as he watched me perfect my jump shot.

The rim was raised every so often, as I grew.

And then one day a girl appeared in my backyard. She had blond hair and a smile that seemed to last forever.

'I live down the street,' she said. 'I'm in your class.'

I kept shooting and hoped that she'd go away. Her name was Erin and she seemed really nice, but I didn't want to make friends with anyone. I only wanted to shoot hoops alone for the rest of my life.

'Are you ignoring me?' she asked.

I tried to pretend she wasn't there, because back then I was pretending the whole world wasn't there.

'You're really weird,' she said. 'But I don't mind.'

My shot clanked off the rim and headed straight for her face, but the girl's reflexes were good and she caught the ball just before it smashed into her nose.

'Do you mind if I take a shot?' she asked.

When I didn't answer, she fired and the ball went in.

'I play a little with my older brother,' she explained.

Whenever I shot around with my dad, the shooter got the ball back after a made basket, so I passed the ball to her and she shot again, and then again, and again.

In my memory, she hits dozens of shots before I get the ball back, but she doesn't ever leave my backyard – the two of us keep shooting for years and years.

PRE-SEASON

'A question that sometimes drives me hazy: Am I or are the others crazy?'

Albert Einstein

ONE

One week before our senior year of high school begins, Erin's wearing her basketball practice jersey and I can see her black sports bra through the armhole, which is sort of sexy, at least to me.

I try not to look – especially since we're eating breakfast with my family – but whenever Erin leans forward and raises her fork to her mouth, her right armhole opens up, and I can see the shape of her small breast perfectly.

Stop looking! I tell myself, but it's impossible.

I don't hear one word that's said over our eggs and sausage.

No one notices my staring.

Erin's so charismatic and beautiful that my dad and pop never pay any attention to me when my girlfriend's around.

Like mine, their eyes are always on Erin.

When we get up to leave, my legless pop yells from

his wheelchair, 'Make the few remaining Irish people in this town proud!'

My father says, 'Just do your best. Remember – it's a long race and you can always outwork talent in the end.'

That's Dad's personal life motto, even though he ended up alone and working the night shift, collecting tolls at the bridge, where he needs neither talent nor a good work ethic.

Mostly because of Pop, my father's life has been pretty dreary. But his eyes always seem hopeful when he says that I can outwork talent over the long haul, and so for him – and for me too – I try my best to do just that.

The nights Dad watches me play basketball, I truly believe that those are the best in his entire life. That's one reason I love b-ball so much: for the opportunity to make Dad happy.

If I've had a good game, Dad's eyes water when he says he's proud of me, which makes my eyes water too.

When Pop sees us like that he calls us pansies.

'You ready?' Erin says to me.

Even though I don't want to, when I look at her face and into her beautiful shamrock-green eyes, I think about kissing her later tonight, and I begin to stiffen, so I quickly wipe the thought out of my mind.

It's not time for romance – it's time to get strong, and basketball season's only two months away.

TWO

Something you maybe need to know: people call me White Rabbit.

Whenever they serve cooked carrots in the lunchroom, Terrell Patterson sneaks up behind me and yells 'Feed White Rabbit!' as he dumps his carrots on my plate as a joke, and then everyone follows his example, until there's a huge mound of orange.

This started last spring.

The first time it happened, I got really mad because people kept walking by and scraping what they didn't want onto my tray, which wasn't very sanitary, especially since I hadn't finished eating my lunch.

Erin – who sits next to me in the cafeteria when it's not basketball season – just started eating the carrots off my plate enthusiastically and thanking people until they got confused.

She kept saying, 'Delicious! May I please have some more!' all crazily, until people were laughing at *her* instead of at what everyone was doing to me.

I actually like carrots, so I ate some too, because I saw that Erin's plan was working and I don't really care that people laugh when I eat those orange vegetables. *I'll have better eyesight than everyone*, I thought, and then just left it at that.

The only problem is that the carrot dumping became a weekly event, and it's really not funny anymore. I hope people forgot about it over the summer, but I doubt it.

I'm one of the few dozen white kids at my high school. I'm quiet like a rabbit. Eminem's character in the movie *8 Mile* is nicknamed B-Rabbit; Eminem is the most famous white rapper in the world; and I actually sort of look like him.

But the main reason people call me White Rabbit is because we had to read this very sad book by John Updike. It was about a long-ago white basketball star named Rabbit who grows up and lives a miserable life. I'm not a star, but I *am* the only white kid on our varsity basketball team.

Wes, who plays center and is the only other basketball player in the Accelerated English track, told all my teammates about the Updike book – well, just the part about there being a white basketball player with an embarrassing name. My teammates all started calling me White Rabbit.

The nickname stuck and now everyone in the neighborhood calls me that too.

THREE

Erin and I grab our basketballs out of the garage, and on my backyard hoop, we each shoot one hundred free throws. It's our last high school basketball season – last shot – so we train hard.

Simulating game situations, we take two shots at a time and box each other out for rebounds. Erin goes eighty-eight for one hundred and I go ninety for one hundred.

Next we jog our five miles, dribbling our basketballs the whole time.

We do a mile of right-hand dribbling down O'Shea Street past a line of row homes that are as broken and gray as Pop's teeth, which gets us to the school, where we continue running the next four miles on the old crappy track that actually has weeds growing up through the lanes. Every lap we dribble a different way – left-handed, crossover, behind the back. We pretty much practice every way you can legally dribble a basketball.

All the other basketball players in our school are also on the football or cheerleading teams, which practice on the fields next to the track, but they aren't practicing yet this early in the morning. Erin wouldn't be caught dead in a cheerleading uniform and I'm not talented enough to play more than one sport successfully. Besides, I want to give my all to basketball.

When we finish, we're soaked in sweat. Little strands of blond hair stick to Erin's face, and her cute little ears have turned red. I really like it when she takes off her practice jersey so that she's only wearing the sports bra. Her bellybutton is a beautiful mystery.

We take a short break as we wait for the school to open up, because the custodians are late again. My muscles are warm and my body feels loose.

We don't talk much.

Erin's one of the few people I know who is okay with silence and, since I don't like talking, it makes us a perfect match. I don't stutter or anything like that. I just *choose* not to speak so much.

We sit in the grass silently for a time.

'You think girls'll win states again this year?' Erin asks me, because she feels pressured to repeat.

What she's really asking is if I think she's good enough to carry her team all the way to another state championship, because our other star girls' player – Keisha Powell – graduated last year and now plays for the Tennessee Lady

Vols. None of the other remaining girls' basketball players are even half as good as Erin.

Concern wrinkles her forehead, so I nod and smile enthusiastically.

Erin's probably the best girls' player in the state – no exaggeration.

When they're being crude, which is always, my team-mates sometimes say that if Erin had a penis (they use a different word), I'd be riding the bench, which isn't the nicest thing to say, but when I watch her dominate a game I sometimes do wonder if my girlfriend actually could beat me out for my position, which is saying a lot.

I know I'm probably not going to play college ball anywhere, not even at the division-three level. I'm a role player on my team, not a star. I'm okay with that. But Erin has a real chance to make a good college team and earn a scholarship, which is another reason I love training and playing off-season b-ball so much: it's a chance to help Erin.

We just want to get the hell out of this town somehow – together – and Erin's basketball career might be our best shot. We talk about leaving Bellmont all the time, moving past the history of our families, breaking free. We've seen too many people make mistakes and get stuck here – like Erin's brother, Rod, and my pop did.

Sitting there on the grass, looking at her beautiful stomach, I start to think about making out with Erin, running my hands up and down her abs. **So I have** to think about where my pop's legs end just below the thigh – his stumps, because that always wipes the sexy thoughts from my mind – and, just like that, my head's right by the time the custodian opens the gym door and says we can come in.

Inside the gym, we run all sorts of sprints and shooting drills and practice free throws.

And then we go out to the stadium and run up and down the steps for twenty minutes of chest-pounding, muscle-screaming, lung-burning action.

Back in the gym we're shooting more patterns when the football team comes in for a bathroom and water break.

Terrell Patterson – chief carrot dumper, starting quarterback, and star shooting guard – yells out from the pack of football players, 'Yo, White Rabbit, why you practicin' your jump shot, boy? You ain't never gonna shoot in a game. You know this! Your job is to get me the ball. Period.'

In between shots, I point to Terrell and smile.

I'm the point guard so it's my job to get the ball to the scorers. Terrell averaged twenty-three points a game last year, and I racked up many assists by feeding him. He probably wouldn't say I'm his friend, but he's my teammate and so I consider him a brother.

I've been the starting point guard for two years now.

Terrell smiles, pounds his fist against his chest two times, and then flashes me the peace sign.

'How you doin', White Rabbit's lil baby?' Terrell yells to Erin, which makes all the football players laugh.

Erin gives Terrell a dirty look and yells, 'I'm not anyone's *lil baby*, Terrell!'

'Damn! The girl mad at me! Shoot!' Terrell says, making everyone laugh again, and then they all follow their coaches into the locker room.

Erin's passes are harder and crisper after Terrell leaves, which lets me know she's upset.

When I finish the pattern, she strides out of the gym even though we still have more shooting patterns to do.

I follow her into the shade underneath the stadium and give her a look that says, *What's wrong?*

'You know I don't like to be called lil baby,' she says.

Her face is tomato red and her forehead is all angry wrinkles.

She looks like she might start punching walls.

'You really have no idea why I'm upset, do you?' she says.

I open my mouth, but – like usual – no words will come.

I don't know what to say.

'There are times when you need to open your mouth more, Finley.'

It's true. Erin isn't saying I need to change my personality, but just stick up for her when it is necessary.

16

I say I'm sorry with my eyes – blinking a lot.

Erin sighs. Then she smiles and there are no more wrinkles in her forehead. Sometimes I'm amazed by how easily she seems to accept me.

'Come on,' she says. 'Let's finish the patterns.'

So we finish our routine and hit the weights before the football team enters the weight room and starts grunting and trying to see who can bench-press the most L-B-S-es.

FOUR

Down at the playground everyone fouls and shoots too much and never allows plays to develop, but Erin and I make sure we're always on the same team so we can work on the things that serious players need to work on, like playing help defense and executing set plays on offense too.

Even though most of the playground players are grown-ups who play ball every day instead of working a job, Erin and I usually beat these men easily, which they hate, mostly because I'm a weird minimal speaker and Erin's a girl.

Only seven or so blocks from our homes, drug dealers hang out by the town courts and old men sit around drinking from brown paper bags. There are crack vials and used syringes strewn about the concrete that surrounds the playground. It's not the safest place in the world, but we are under the protection of Erin's brother, Rod.

Rod is in his late twenties, plays drums in a Pogues-type, Irish-trad-punk band, and, if the rumors are true, deals a little himself, only not on the streets. But the important part is that his reputation proclaims him to be the most unpredictable and violent Irishman ever to live in Bellmont. Neighborhood people are scared of him, and rightly so.

Once when we were freshmen there was this upperclassman named Don Little who had a thing for Erin. He followed her around school and talked sexy to her. I'm not even going to repeat some of the things he used to say because they are so horrifically base. Whenever I would hear Don Little say something lewd to Erin, my chest would get tight and my hands would ball up into fists, but, of course, my tongue wouldn't work at all.

Don Little was a nineteen-year-old senior who had been in juvie for dealing cocaine and Erin was a fourteen-year-old kid.

One day Erin and I were walking home, and Don Little followed us and when we were far enough away from the high school he grabbed Erin's butt and said some really lewd things.

It was like I wasn't even there – or I didn't matter. I was so mad that I tried to say something, but all that came out was 'Heyahhhh!'

Don Little laughed and said, 'Why don't you ditch the retard and get with a real man?'

That's when I charged him. But before I could land any punches, he dropped me with one punch to the jaw.

BAAAMMMMM!

POP!

STARS!

I remember my legs flying up in the air, seeing clouds above, and then blacking out.

When I came around, Erin was stroking my cheek, saying, 'Wake up! Come on, Finley, wake up!'

Her nose was bleeding. Warm heavy drops were hitting my neck.

'What happened?' I asked.

'I beat Don Little's ass.'

'What?'

'I punched him in the face after he hit you. I was so pissed!'

'Your nose.'

'Yeah, he got in a good shot before he ran away.'

'Are you okay?'

'Are you?'

'I think so.'

'Well, then, me too.'

She helped me up and walked me home and I asked her not to tell anyone about her defending me from Don Little, which made her laugh.

'You mean you're not proud of your girlfriend's ability to kick ass?' she asked.

I puked on the sidewalk in response, and immediately felt less woozy.

Erin's brother, Rod, visited me later that night.

I hadn't seen him in a long time, because he no longer lived with the Quinns.

He had been lifting weights and looked like a professional bodybuilder. He was wearing a tight T-shirt with skulls on it and black jeans rolled up so that you could see the white laces of his black Doc Martens boots. His head was shaved and his arms were covered with Celtic tattoos.

'Mr McManus, you mind if I speak to your boy alone?' Rod asked.

'Why alone?' Dad asked. 'We're family.'

'I think you know why,' Rod said.

Dad and Rod stared at each other for a few seconds until Rod said, 'I put in good words for you and your family, but people don't forget.'

Dad's face turned white and I started to feel sick when I saw that the gray hair around his temples was slick with sweat.

'We don't want any trouble,' Dad said.

'Then leave us alone for a few minutes. Your boy's a good kid. We know that. We're only trying to help.'

I was surprised that my father actually left and shut the door behind him.

Rod asked me what had transpired, so I told him what I remembered.

He grabbed the back of my head and carefully pulled my forehead closer to his, so that our eyebrows were touching. His eyelashes brushed up against mine whenever he blinked. The liquor on his breath was dank and smelled sharp as a razor blade. 'After tonight, brother, no one in this neighborhood will touch you or my sister ever again. I promise you that.'

The next morning they found Don Little unconscious on the town basketball court. His entire body was swollen and bruised.

His braids had been cut and his head shaved.

I heard there was a sign around his neck that read I HIT GIRLS.

The cops investigated, but neither Don Little nor anyone else ever said a word about what everyone assumed to be true.

Most people don't snitch to the police around here.

Don Little dropped out of school and left town shortly after, and no one in Bellmont has ever laid a finger on Erin or me since.

This is why we can play pickup basketball at the town courts without being harassed by the criminals who hang around there. We know that if Rod were not around, we'd be treated differently, which makes me sort of sad.

FIVE

In front of her house – a brick row home under a faded and ripped yellow awning – Erin says that she'll be over just as soon as she's showered, and then she kisses me once on the lips before disappearing behind the front screen door.

I jog the one block home down O'Shea Street.

The neighborhood is gray and dingy and littered with trash, but all the row homes are occupied and therefore not condemned, so our blocks look pretty healthy compared to most around here.

When I cross the street to my block, I notice Coach Wilkins's old Ford pickup truck parked in front of our house.

Coach has come to pay me a visit and he's now alone inside my house with Pop, who sometimes gets drunk during the day and starts dancing with family skeletons – talking freely about stuff I don't want anyone to know, especially Coach.

I sprint into my house and yell, 'Coach?'

'Finley, I'm right here. No need to yell.' He's wearing a summer suit with no tie and fancy shoes. Why's he dressed up?

He's on the sofa in the living room. My pop's wheelchair is parked next to the couch and thankfully Pop looks relatively sober.

'Coach Wilkins would like to take you out to dinner,' Pop says. He's in a wife-beater undershirt and his tan pants are pinned under his stumps. Pop's white hair is tucked behind his ears and falls to his shoulders. He's not trying to look cool with the long hair; he just doesn't care enough to make the trip to the barber. Grandmom's green rosary beads make a *V* on Pop's chest and Jesus hangs on a black cross right around Pop's outie bellybutton.

'To a friend's house, actually,' Coach says. And then, noticing how sweaty I am, he adds, 'Looks like you've been working out pretty hard today.'

'With Erin Quinn,' Pop says. 'That's his lady friend.'

'She's a fine ball player and a fine young woman,' Coach says. 'So, Finley.'

I like the fact that Coach doesn't call me White Rabbit, especially since my teammates are always trying to get him to use the nickname.

Coach says, 'You want to dine with me tonight?'

I nod.

I do whatever Coach asks of me. He's my coach.

'Why don't you shower up and we'll talk about it on the way. And wear something nice,' Coach says.

'I'll be needing your assistance before you go,' Pop says.

I push Pop's wheelchair into the bathroom, where I quickly help him change his soiled diaper.

When we return to the living room my father's up. (Dad sleeps days and works nights.) He and Coach are talking hoops and smiling so I park Pop next to them. Pop says, 'Hurry your ass up,' as I jog up the steps.

In the shower I wonder where Coach is taking me.

He's never asked me to dinner and he's only visited my home twice before. Once after I was beat up by Don Little, and once after I hurt my ankle sophomore year.

I can't imagine where he would be taking me tonight, but I'm excited to find out.

SIX

I pull on my black trousers and my light blue shirt with the collar and three buttons, and then Coach and I are walking out the door as my father's telling me to mind my manners. He's standing in the doorway looking tired but wearing the hopeful we-have-guests face that he puts on whenever anyone other than Pop and me is around.

With her hair still wet, Erin walks up to the house wearing a colorful summer dress. She and Coach say hello.

'You mind if I borrow Finley for a few hours?' Coach asks.

'Not at all,' Erin says, but when she catches my eyes I can tell she's a little bummed, and definitely confused, so I shrug to let her know I have no idea what's going on. I want to hang out with Erin, but I see her every night. Plus, she understands that when your coach pays a house visit, it means that something important is happening. Erin says, 'Coach, when'll you be returning Finley?'

'I'd say we'll be back by nine or so.'

'See you then,' Erin says to me, and then she starts walking home.

'You're lucky to have a friend like Erin,' Coach says as we get into his truck and buckle up. 'People need friends. *Real friends* – like Erin is to you.'

The engine rumbles to life and the air-conditioning hits me in the face.

It feels really cool, but Coach doesn't drive.

His face is dark and strong as always, but he keeps swallowing. His Adam's apple is going up and down, so I know something is wrong.

Coach says, 'You know how I'm always telling the team that basketball can teach you a lot about life and that those lessons are more important than wins and losses and personal stats, more important than the game itself – that we're learning life lessons on the court and that's the most important part of the experience?'

'Yeah.'

Coach is always saying that.

'Well, I think you're going to learn a lot this year, Finley.'

Something about the way he says those words makes me feel sort of strange. Like he's trying to be prophetic

27

or something, and this dinner's even more important than I originally thought.

I look at Coach's face and try to read his eyes. I see desperation, frustration, exhaustion – what I see in the eyes of all the men who have lived in this neighborhood for too many years.

'We've got a bit of a situation here, Finley. Because I trust you, I'm gonna tell you a lot tonight and I want you to keep it all confidential. You can tell no one what I'm about to say. Not your dad or grandfather or Erin. Not your teammates. And especially no one at school. Can I trust you to keep this information top secret?'

I can't imagine what Coach is going to tell me.

My heart's beating really hard, and I realize that I'm swallowing now too.

I nod to let Coach know that I'll keep the secret.

'Okay then. Does the name Russell Allen mean anything to you?'

I shake my head.

'Here's the secret: Russell Allen played his first three years of high-school ball out in LA. He gained a national reputation last year as a junior. Quite simply, he's one of the top recruits in the country. At seventeen he already has the body of a professional ball player. I've seen game tapes and I'm convinced he could play for any NBA team right now. He's a six-five point guard who can play inside and out. Smart player. Can run an offense. Rebounds.

Hustles. The best high-school defender I have ever seen. And to top it off, he scored near perfect on his SATs and was able to maintain a four-point-oh GPA through three years of all-season basketball. He's played in all the best camps. He's been outgoing and trouble-free all through high school. Great work ethic. Every collegiate program in the country wants the kid.'

It's clear that Coach loves this player, but I can't figure out why he's telling me all this – especially if Allen plays on the other side of the country – let alone why I need to keep it a secret.

'You know the Allens over on Porter Street, by that dive bar called Drinkers?'

'No.' I never go to that part of town. There are no Irish there.

'Those folks are Russell Allen's grandparents and good friends of mine. I used to play ball with Russell's father, Russell senior. He ended up becoming a pretty well-known jazz musician, a saxophonist. He moved to LA and started writing music for movies. Made enough money to put Russell into a real good prep school out there, where he did pretty well until—'

Coach is gripping the steering wheel too hard and licking his lips repetitively.

I've never seen Coach get nervous like this before.

'My friend Russell and his wife were murdered last February.' The word *murdered* gets stuck in my ear and suddenly it feels like someone is jabbing a finger into my throat. I begin to cough a little, but Coach keeps talking. It takes a few minutes for my mind to process the rest of his words. 'The details aren't important right now. But the event has had a dramatic effect on Russell junior. He's spent some time in a group home for kids who suffer from post-traumatic stress. The Allens here in town are his closest relatives and even though they don't feel quite up to taking on a troubled teenage boy, because Russell requested it, they have agreed to care for him until he goes to college next year.'

I suddenly realize that Russell will be eligible to play for our basketball team. And even though Coach is talking about the aftereffects of a murder, I'm ashamed to admit that I immediately begin worrying about my starting position. It's like being told I have cancer and might need a part of me removed – the part called starting point guard.

'So,' I say, 'he's going to play for us, Coach?'

'Well, I hope he *will* come out for the team, but at this point his mental health is what we need to be focusing on. He hasn't touched a basketball in months. You see, after all that's happened, Russell's not really right in the head. We all think that a boy with his gifts should be using them and, with so many colleges ready to give him a full ride, it would be a shame to watch him sit the season out, but we need to take one thing at a time, which is why he's going to enroll under his mother's maiden name. The Allens don't want college scouts and coaches bothering Russell until he moves past his issues. The basketball world doesn't know he's here. And he's not exactly interested in basketball right now. *Understand*?'

I have no idea why I'm in the truck.

I'm lost.

'I've told them that our high school can be rough and Russell would be better off in a private school, especially since he's inherited a lot of money. But, for some reason, the Allens want the boy to play basketball for me this year. Probably because they know me, and after all that's happened, they don't want to put Russell into the hands of a stranger. So under the name Russ Washington, Russell is going to transition to our school, which couldn't be any more different from the prep school he attended in California. Administration, his guidance counselor, me, and now you – those are the only people who'll know Russell's true identity. Okay?'

I don't know what to say. I really don't.

Coach says, 'I thought that maybe if Russell had a friend who knew what it was like to be *different*, the transition might be a little easier.'

Suddenly, I think I might understand my role.

'You have a question on your face, Finley. Now's the time to ask it.'

Even though I know that the Allens live in an

all-black section of town, I say, 'So, Coach, are you saying Russell's white?'

'Does the color of his skin matter?' Coach asks.

He's always saying that he doesn't see the color of a man's skin, but I know that's just politically correct talk. Coach absolutely changes his game plan depending on the opposing team's skin color, because black and white teams usually play different styles of basketball, and that's just a fact.

When I don't say anything, Coach says, 'Russell's pretty much the same color as I am.'

'Then why *me*?' I ask.

'Well, let's just say that I have a hunch you two will get along. That and you're pretty much the only boy on the team I trust to help my dead friend's son.'

Those words make me swallow hard.

Part of me just wants to be with Erin, and yet, another part of me's intrigued, kind of flattered, and a little nervous, all at once.

Coach shifts into gear and drives us across town to the Allens' house.

SEVEN

When he parks, Coach says, 'There's one other thing.'

He gets this look on his face like he has to use the bathroom or something. He looks way uncomfortable. He's strangling the steering wheel.

'Russell isn't exactly going by the name Russell at this moment in his life.' Coach glances out the windshield with this vacant look on his face. 'Russell now likes to be called Boy21.' He nods a few times, as if to say he isn't joking.

'Why?' I say, noting that twenty-one is my basketball number. Could this night possibly get any weirder?

'The people at his group home and his local therapist have both recommended that we all call him Boy21 out of respect for his wishes. They say he now needs to exert control over his environment in some small way, or something like that. I don't know anything about therapy, but I think after all that's happened the boy could sure use a kindhearted friend. That's what this is about. We'll call him Boy21 tonight and work on getting him back to Russ before school starts.'

I nod, but I imagine my expression says something different. Am I kindhearted? How can I be a friend to this kid when I don't really even talk to people, and I don't have any true friends besides Erin? Will he want my basketball number?

Coach's eyebrows are pushing the skin on his forehead into folds and he's swallowing every five seconds now.

He reaches across the truck, puts his hand on my shoulder, and says, 'I'm doing this out of respect for my late friend. And, Finley, no matter how this goes, thank you for coming. You're a good kid. I'm only asking you to give tonight a shot. Nothing more. If it doesn't go well, we'll just forget about it. *Okay?*'

'Okay.'

'Well. Here we go.'

We get out of Coach's truck. The Allens' street is much worse than mine. Broken bottles and fast-food wrappers litter the sidewalks, a few houses are boarded up, and just about every building is tagged with graffiti curse words, but the Allens' place is actually pretty nice. The lawn's cut, the bushes are shaped, and the house itself looks well kept and inviting. It's even been freshly painted, which is a rare sight in Bellmont.

Coach rings the doorbell and soon a white-haired couple answers.

'Timothy!' The old woman is wearing a black dress. She wraps her arms around Coach's neck so that he has to bend over. 'Thank you so much for coming.'

'Pleasure, Ms Allen.'

Mr Allen – who's wearing a gray suit – shakes Coach's hand very formally and says, 'Thank you again for what you said at the funeral. You're a poet, a good friend, and a kind soul.'

'I only spoke the truth,' Coach says. Everyone's eyes are suddenly glistening. 'This here's Finley McManus. One of the finest young men on my ball squad. Good people here. I promise you that.'

I'm a little embarrassed by Coach's introduction, but I'm also a little proud.

Mr Allen looks at me and says, 'Thanks for coming.'

I know Mr Allen is probably surprised that I'm white, but that doesn't bother me. I'd probably be surprised if I were him too. Actually, I'm surprised that Coach picked me for this job. I'm not a therapist, nor do I have much in common with the Allen family at all. They're probably thinking I won't be able to relate to their grandson, that I might even be a liability for him in the new neighborhood, and I completely agree. Black kids with white best friends are not common in Bellmont. Maybe that's blunt, but I've found that being blunt sometimes makes life easier for everyone.

'Come in,' Mrs Allen says.

EIGHT

It's air-conditioned inside.

Pictures of Jesus hang all around the house. Jesus cuddling lambs. Jesus in a garden. Jesus wearing a purple robe. The furniture is very old, but the rooms are the cleanest I've ever been in. Everything wooden is polished, the rugs are fluffy and freshly vacuumed, and you couldn't find a single speck of dust even if you moved around the picture frames. It's like being in a museum, compared to our messy man-house.

I'm sitting next to Coach on the couch when Mrs Allen hands me a glass of lemonade.

'So where's Russ?' Coach says.

'Up in his room,' Mr Allen says. 'I'm afraid I couldn't get him to come down. I told him you were coming, but, well, you see' – he lowers his voice here – 'the social worker told us that we shouldn't push the boy just yet, but let him acclimate to the new setting, so—'

'Would you go up and talk with him?' Mrs Allen asks me.

She's a tiny thin lady, but her eyes are forceful, piercing, so I simply nod because I always do what my elders ask of me. That's how Pop and Dad raised me.

'Might as well let the boys meet,' Mr Allen says a little too hopefully, as if he's trying to hide his true expectations, but maybe I'm just being paranoid.

'You okay with that, Finley?' Coach says, resting his hand on my shoulder again.

I nod.

A good ball player always listens to his coach, especially when his coach is as smart as mine.

'Upstairs, second door on your left,' Mrs Allen says.

I place my glass on a coaster and stand.

'Did you tell him about the outer-space fixation?' Mr Allen says to Coach.

When I give Coach a questioning glance, he says, 'Go on upstairs, Finley. Say hello. Okay?'

I wonder what any of this has to do with outer space, but Coach's eyes beg me not to ask him anything in front of the Allens, so I don't.

As I walk across the room and make my way to the stairs, I can feel my elders watching me, but once I'm out of sight I go slowly and study the pictures on the wall that leads up to the second floor, trying to figure out just what kind of a mess I'm in.

There are black-and-white pictures of Mr and Mrs Allen taken when they were young, and I recognize different corners of Bellmont even though the cars and clothing styles are outdated and the town looks much cleaner and safer.

There's an old wedding picture and Coach is the best man; he's rocking a huge Afro, wearing a powder-blue tuxedo, and looking more like my classmates than an adult, which makes me smile.

The photos of Boy21 begin when he was a baby and go all the way to the present day.

It's obvious his family had money. His clothing looks expensive in all the school photos, and there are pictures of him and his parents taken in foreign places: in front of the Eiffel Tower and also that leaning tower in Italy – even one by those pyramids in Egypt.

I start to feel a little jealous of this kid, because I've never been anywhere but Bellmont and he's been all over the world, which doesn't really seem fair. Why is it that some people are born into fantastic situations and others wait their whole lives for a break?

Russell's smiling nicely in all of the shots. He looks like a good kid, which makes it hard for me to hate him.

And then I see his high-school basketball team photo: he's the only black kid. His squad's wearing cool brand-new Nike uniforms, like a college team. They even have matching sneakers.

Maybe Coach knew that Boy21 was the only black kid on his team like I'm the only white kid on my team, and that's why Coach picked me for this job.

But I also see Russ is wearing number 21 – my number – and I can't help but feel threatened.

At the top of the steps there are no more pictures. I walk down the hall, where an entire room's contents are in boxes. I have to turn sideways as I pass a big chest of drawers and a desk. A mattress and bed frame are leaning against the wall.

Behind the only closed door in the hallway, someone is talking.

I put my ear up to the door and hear a man's voice say, 'Perseus! Perseus the hero! Slayer of Medusa! There you are, my friend! A road map to a new existence. Space is the place! Space is the place!'

Whoever is behind the door sounds absolutely insane.

But for Coach, I do as I was instructed to do.

Good basketball players execute the game plan.

Always.

I raise my fist and knock.

NINE

The voice stops talking and after a long few seconds the door opens inward and I'm looking up at a shirtless man-child.

His body is incredible.

The perfect basketball body.

Tall, lean, strong – it looks exactly like Kobe Bryant's.

He has four-inch braids that are unlike what my teammates wear – those neat Manny Ramirez braids. Boy21's braids are so nappy, they almost look like Bob Marley's dreads.

'You are an Earthling?' Boy21 says to me.

I swallow and nod.

'I am programmed to treat all Earthlings with kindness. Greetings. I am Boy21 from the cosmos. I am stranded here on Earth, but I will be leaving soon. Enter into my domestic living pod.'

He turns his back on me and resumes what he was doing.

I step into the empty room and see that the ceiling and walls have recently been painted black.

Books are open all over the floor. They're all about outer space. Hundreds of constellations and galaxies and universes are spread out at my feet.

When I look up, Boy21 has a book in his hand and is arranging constellations on the wall using those glow-in-the-dark plastic stars – what little kids stick on their bedroom ceilings.

He's already filled an entire wall with constellations.

'I just finished Perseus. That there is Algol – the demon star. This here is pretend outer space – or fantasy outer space – so we're not really interested in arranging the constellations the way they usually appear.' His expression is blank – completely alien. 'We're just putting up our favorites so we'll feel more at home in our domestic pod here on Earth. What's *your* favorite constellation? And do you have a name, Earthling?'

This isn't a game or a joke. He's crazy.

'Earthling, is your audio intake system damaged? Can you hear me, Earthling?'

'Um . . .' is all I can manage. What am I supposed to say to this insane kid who thinks he's from space?

'Is your audio output system damaged? What you

42

English-speaking Earthlings call *the tongue* – is yours working?'

'Yeah.'

'So you are just *parsimonious* with your words?'

'Parsimonious. Yeah. I guess.' I note the proper use of the SAT word. Is this some sort of game? Is Coach playing a practical joke?

'I respect your parsimonious nature,' he says, and then continues arranging constellations his own way as he mumbles facts about outer space.

I don't know what to say, so I say nothing, like always.

After five minutes or so, Boy21 turns and says, 'Is it okay if I call you by your Earthling name – Finley?'

His grandparents probably told him my name, but his using it without my telling him what it is sort of surprises me.

'May I?' he says.

'Sure.' What the hell is with this kid?

'My name is Boy21. I'm a prototype. A test model. I was sent to your planet temporarily to gather scientific information on what you Earthlings know as emotions. But I will only be with you for a few more months. Soon my makers will come for me and take me back into the cosmos, where I will be studied and disassembled and ultimately freed. I realize that these are strange ideas and are therefore probably hard for your brain to process, because you are merely an Earthling. So perhaps we should nourish your system with sustenance at this juncture?'

I just look at him blankly.

'Would you like to consume atoms?' he says. 'What you refer to as *eating dinner*.'

Realizing that this will get me back into the company of sane people, I nod. 'I'm starving.'

'Very well,' he says, and then slips into a white undershirt on which he has written with Magic Markers.

The rainbow lettering on his shirt reads:

N.A.S.A.
(Nubians Are Superior Astronauts)

'Do you like my shirt, Earthling known as Finley?' he asks when he sees me looking at it. 'Black man and the cosmos. Two great things that go great together.'

I'm speechless.

He says, 'Am I not using your Earthling language effectively?'

Holy crap. What on earth is going on here?

Boy21 smiles knowingly and says something with his eyes that I don't quite understand.

When he descends the stairs I follow and somehow I find myself eating a delicious meal with Coach, Boy21, and the Allens.

Roast beef.

String beans.

Garlic mashed potatoes.

None of the adults say anything about Boy21's shirt, and he remains silent through the entire meal.

'How're you liking Bellmont so far?' Coach asks.

'Russell,' Mr Allen says. 'Coach is talking to you.'

'It's okay,' Coach says. 'You don't have to talk if you don't want to. There will be time for talking.'

All the adults exchange glances, and I'm glad that they don't glance at me.

'You like the food?' Mrs Allen says.

'Yes. Thank you,' I say, and then it's just the sounds of knives and forks scraping against the plates, chewing, swallowing, glasses of water being sipped and set down on wood.

Boy21 keeps his eyes on his food until it's gone, which is when he says, 'May I take Finley back up to my room?'

'Are you finished eating?' Mrs Allen asks me.

I nod, even though I'm not, and say, 'Thanks.'

'You boys go have your fun,' Coach says, and then I'm back in Boy21's room watching him arrange glow-in-the-dark sticker constellations.

'You don't talk much, do you?' Boy21 asks, looking over his shoulder.

'No.'

'Did something happen to you?' he asks.

Truth is, many things have happened to me, both

good and bad, stuff that would take a lot of words to explain, too many words for me.

There's a part of me that wants to discuss my past, why I don't talk much, outer space even, everything, but it's like my mind is a fist and it's always clenched tight, trying to keep the words in.

Boy21 faces me and says, 'Do you believe I'm from outer space?'

I shrug.

'You will when I ascend, but until then I'll need someone to help me complete my mission here on Earth. You seem like you are quite emotional, and I am very interested in studying emotions. Are you trustworthy?'

I nod, because I'm generally trustworthy, but I also smile, because I'm not emotional at all. At least, I try not to be.

He smiles back.

'Will you show me the ways of your culture?' he asks, and then adds, 'Please.'

'You playing basketball this year?'

Boy21 turns his back on me and says, 'I am programmed to be an excellent basketball player. No Earthling can beat me. But I think I'll be long gone before the season rolls around. I'll be back in the cosmos well before the time period that you Earthlings call November.'

I feel relieved when he says this because if he's gone

by November, it means he'll miss basketball season, and then I remind myself how crazy this whole situation is.

He's absolutely nuts.

There's no way he'd be able to get through the demands of an organized basketball season, especially claiming to be from outer space. Basketball is a game of rules that you must submit to for the good of the team, and Boy21 is already not playing by the rules.

I start to think about what's going to happen to Russell if he pretends to be from outer space once school starts.

At lunch he'll be relegated to my table. Students will dump carrots on his plate.

I don't like the way things are in Bellmont.

'You can't tell people you're from outer space,' I say.

'Why not?' he says with a genuinely curious look on his face. 'Do people enjoy hearing mistruths in this sector of Earth?'

Bellmont's too complicated for me to explain in a sentence. The drugs, the violence, the racial tension, the Irish mob – how do you explain who runs the town when you could get killed just for saying the words *Irish mob*? I keep my mouth shut.

Boy21 faces me and says, 'Why do you care about what happens to *me*, Earthling?'

I shrug, but then I say, 'I guess I just sort of care about *everyone*.'

He smiles at me – I know this will sound weird but

his expression sort of warms my chest, removes the jabbing finger from my throat; his teeth sparkle and wink – and then he returns to his glow-in-the-dark stickers.

I sit down on the floor and watch him arrange constellations. He peels off the little dots of two-sided tape, places a sticky dot in the center of each star, places the star on the end of his forefinger, and then presses it onto the wall or ceiling. He hops into the air like Superman to affix the stars above him, and lands gracefully without shaking the house too much, mostly because he's so tall that he doesn't have to leap that high, but also because he's obviously athletic. There's a very determined look on his face – it's like his eyebrows are trying to meet for the first time at the top of his nose.

After ten minutes or so, he pulls the blinds, turns out the lights, and sits next to me.

'Pretend you are in outer space,' he says.

It's so absurd; I almost want to laugh.

I have no idea what it's like to be in outer space, but I know that I've never felt quite like I do at this very moment. Maybe I should feel scared or at least alarmed, but Boy21 seems pretty harmless, so I just sit and stare.

What else can I do?

After a few minutes of absolute quiet, I think about why Boy21 might be arranging stars in his bedroom. Maybe he likes being in control of his own little universe, being able to arrange things how he wants, like a god or something? Maybe he likes pretending, like a little kid would. I'm not sure, but I don't mind either.

The only other person I have ever sat alone with in the dark is Erin, and since I always want to kiss her, I never get to just enjoy the quiet shared silence.

It's nice to sit with another person, although I'm not sure why.

As crazy as this will sound, I'm really enjoying just being with Boy21.

There aren't many people my age who will join me in voluntary silence. Most kids in my high school talk nonstop and are always moving.

The stickers glow an otherworldly green and I have to admit that I like looking at them.

We just sit silently for a long time, which feels kind of *right* somehow, even though my skin is sort of tingling in this weird way.

'Boys?' Coach says as he opens the door, letting in the hall light and breaking the spell. 'What are you two doing in the dark?'

'Stargazing, Earthling,' Boy21 says.

'Oh,' Coach says, swiveling his head to admire Boy21's many constellations. 'Time to go, Finley.'

'Where is your dwelling pod, Earthling known as Finley?' Boy21 asks when I stand.

'Five twenty-one O'Shea Street,' I say. 'Across town.'

'I will appear to you later tonight.' Boy21 offers me his hand, which is twice the size of mine.

I shake it and give Boy21 a questioning squint, but then Coach says, 'Nice to see you again, Boy21. I look forward to our next meeting.'

We say good-bye to the Allens and then Coach is driving me home.

Watching the neighborhood go by – the sagging row homes, potholed roads, trash blowing around, tree bark tagged with graffiti – I wonder if Boy21 will really visit me tonight.

Just for a laugh, I imagine him landing in our tiny front yard, maybe in a personal-size flying saucer, which would probably just fill the center circle of a basketball court. His spaceship has a green dome on top that opens up like an Easter egg. 'Hello, Finley!' Boy21 says in my mind. 'Let's go cruise the galaxy!' I have to hide my smile from Coach.

TEN

'So what do you think of Russ?' Coach asks.

Here's what comes to mind: it's like Russ has created a force field of weirdness around himself, but as that sounds like crazy talk, I keep my mouth shut.

'It's a lot to take in at first,' Coach says. 'My guess is that some of it's just an act to keep certain people at bay. I think he might be pretending to protect himself, but what do I know? The boy's been through a lot. I appreciate your coming tonight. Do you think you could maybe show Russ around next week when school starts?'

'Of course.'

'And keep Russell's secret too?'

'Yes, sir.'

When we pull up to my house, Coach shakes my hand and says, 'You're a real good kid, Finley. You do know that, right?'

I smile and hop out of the truck.

Inside Pop's playing War with Erin at the kitchen table. Their stacks of cards are just about even. Pop slams each card like he's trying to karate chop a board in half, while Erin places hers lightly on the table. Whenever Erin wins she says something like, 'Ah, too bad, Mr McManus. Maybe next time, old-timer.' I love it when she's sarcastic. So does Pop. I can tell because of the smile he tries to hide.

'So,' Pop says, 'what's the new kid like?'

I don't know how to answer. I don't want to say how weird he is, and I don't want to betray him by giving away his secrets, so I just shrug.

'Can you believe this dumb mute?' Pop says to Erin. 'Couldn't get a word out of 'im if you beat 'im with a stick.'

'I forfeit. You win, Pop,' Erin says and then leads me by the hand toward my bedroom.

'Get back here, missy! I got all your aces!' Pop says. 'Play it out! This is War!'

But we're already halfway up the stairs.

We open the screen window, hop out onto the roof, and lie down.

We make out for a little while, which feels pretty nice, and then Erin lays her head on my chest and says, 'Did Coach take you to meet a new player?'

'A new student.' I run my fingers through her hair and massage her scalp. She loves that.

'Was he nice?'

'Yeah. He was.'

'What's his name?'

'Boy21.'

Erin laughs, like I'm joking.

So I say, 'Russ Washington.'

And then my hand makes its way down her back and we kiss some more.

When we finish, we don't talk. We just lie there looking up at the half-moon until it's time for me to walk her home.

After gazing into her eyes for what seems like a long time, I kiss Erin good night on her porch, and then leave.

It was an awesome roof night, especially since Erin is a very good kisser, but I'm not thinking about Erin right now. I'm surprised to find myself thinking about Boy21.

I feel weird.

I feel worried.

I feel sorry for Boy21 because his parents were murdered and he thinks he's from outer space, but, then, his knowing so much about constellations is pretty interesting. He seems very smart – intelligent enough to pretend convincingly, which makes me wonder if Coach's theory is correct, if Boy21 is just acting.

What if Boy21 snaps out of it by basketball season?

If he's even half as good as Coach thinks he is, I'll lose my starting position.

And yet Coach picks *me* to help Boy21.

If I help him, I could end up riding the pine this season, and if I don't help Boy21 acclimate to Bellmont, I'd be disobeying Coach for the first time in my life.

Boy21's parents were murdered, I tell myself. *Murdered. Don't be selfish!*

My mind also says, *But this is your senior year, your last season, and Erin and you have worked so hard on your game. . . .*

Does he really truly believe that he's from outer space?

Will he want my number?

I also wonder if we'll maybe end up being friends – *real* friends.

I've never really had a good guy friend.

It's always just been Erin.

Boy21 and I have already sat in silence together, and on the first night we met too.

What was it about the green constellations?

I stop walking.

'I like your dwelling pod,' Boy21 says. He's standing very rigidly in front of my house, like he's really nervous.

'How did you get here?' I ask.

'I have a map for this sector of Earth. I never go anywhere on your planet without a map.'

'Why are you here?'

'I was sent to your planet to gather scientific data on what you Earthlings call emotions.'

'No. Why are you standing in front of my house right now?'

'I saw you lying on your roof. Behind that big tree over there across the street, I politely waited for your love partner to leave.'

I just stare up at Boy21.

He was spying on me, which should freak me out, but for some reason I don't feel angry. I'm mostly curious about why he came to my house at all.

'Can we sit up there together and identify all we see in the cosmos?' he asks, and then points toward the roof.

I don't know why but – suddenly, almost involuntarily – I nod once, and then he follows me into my house.

My dad – who picked up an extra one-to-nine-a.m. Friday-night shift and is therefore leaving for work – says, 'Are you the new kid?'

'Is that the English-language human term you will call me, Earthling?' Boy21 says. *New kid?*

'Did he just call me *Earthling*?' Dad says to me. His expression makes him look uncomfortable, like he's squinting directly into the sun.

I shrug.

'Your grandparents are worried about you,' Dad says

to Boy21, staring in disbelief at the N.A.S.A. T-shirt. 'Coach called asking if you were here. I'll just give him a ring back now to let him know where you are.'

Dad goes into the other room to make the call.

From his wheelchair Pop says, 'The neighborhood people don't know you, son. It's not safe to walk across town at night alone.'

'Nothing on this planet can possibly harm me,' Boy21 says.

Pop says, 'I wish that were true, but it ain't.'

Dad returns and says, 'Coach is coming to pick up Russ. You two can wait out front if you want to talk. But I need to go to work now.'

When my dad leaves, we sit on the front steps and Boy21 says, 'I'd like to sit with you on your roof in the future and teach you about my home – outer space. You have a calming presence, Finley. Would it be possible to sit on your roof with you in the future?'

No one has ever told me that I have a calming presence. Maybe people think it, but they just don't say it. 'Sure,' I say.

I like the words *calming presence* much more than *White Rabbit* or *dumb mute*.

Calming presence.

I search his face, trying to determine if he's making fun of me or being ironic, but he's not – he's one hundred percent serious, or at least I believe he is.

We sit in silence until a tired-looking Coach pulls up ten minutes later, smiles an embarrassed thank-you to me, and takes Russ away in his truck.

I lie awake all night thinking about Boy21.

ELEVEN

The night before school begins Erin and I are making out on my roof when suddenly she pulls away and says, 'Is that Coach's truck?'

I sit up, peer down over the edge of the gutter, and see the old Ford.

'Finley!' Dad yells from the living room.

Erin and I slide through my bedroom window and jog down the stairs.

'Hope I'm not interrupting anything,' Coach says. He and Dad share a smile.

'No,' Erin says. 'Nothing at all.'

'Take a drive with me, Finley?' Coach says.

'Sure thing.'

'We'll only be ten minutes, Erin. Promise,' Coach says.

'No sweat.' Erin plops onto the couch and takes the remote control from Pop's hand, because he's passed-out drunk again with my grandmother's rosary beads wrapped tightly around his left fist like brass knuckles. There's a green Jameson whiskey bottle between his legs. 'I'll just watch some TV with my favorite senior citizen.'

Dad shakes his head at Pop's state, but no one says anything.

As we get into Coach's truck, I see sweat beads on his forehead and dark spots on his shirt where he has sweated through the fabric. It's a hot sticky night, but I can tell Coach is nervous.

He drives me around the block, and then parks with the engine running, the air-conditioning on full blast, which feels nice because we don't have air-conditioning at my house.

'Are you still willing to help Russ?' Coach asks.

I know what he wants me to say, so I say it.

'Good. Here's the situation,' Coach says. 'It took some convincing, but the boy's agreed to stop talking about outer space and go by Russ Washington. No more Boy21 – at least not in school. But given the stress of classes and a new environment, there's no guarantee that he might not slip back into his routine, so I want you to stick by him. I want you by his side every second of the day. If he has to take a leak, you go with him. Understood?'

It sounds like Coach is preparing me to mark a man in a basketball game, because he's raising his voice like he does in huddles. He's being more forceful, and it's like I'm not doing him a favor anymore, but just doing what I am supposed to do as a member of the basketball team. I'm willing to help, but I feel like the circumstances have changed somehow. Or am I just being paranoid?

'What if we're not in the same classes?' I ask.

'Don't worry about that. What time should I tell Mr Allen to drop off Russ?'

'Drop him off where?'

'At your house, so you can walk to school together.'

Erin and I always walk to school together alone, and that's my favorite part of the day. I like talking to Erin first thing in the morning, and kissing her too. I think quick and say, 'Can Mr Allen drop Russ off at Erin's house around seven twenty?'

'Done.'

This way, I can go to Erin's at seven and spend at least twenty minutes with her alone. It'll mean waking up a bit earlier, but I don't mind.

'Finley.'

'Yes.'

Coach reaches over and squeezes my shoulder. 'This Russ – he's special. His doing well here at Bellmont means a lot to me. His father was a close friend.'

I nod.

'You won't let me down, right?'

'No, sir.'

'Good. Seven twenty at Erin's house. What number is hers?'

I actually can't remember, so I say, 'Just a block down the street from mine. We'll be sitting on the front steps. Mr Allen won't be able to miss us.'

'And you didn't tell Erin anything about the situation, right?'

'No more than necessary.'

'Thank you for that. Let's keep Russ's true identity a secret at least until basketball season is under way.'

I want to ask Coach about my starting position – how he can ask me to help the kid who's threatening to take it away – but I don't say anything and Coach drives me home.

When we pull up to my house, he says, 'Just tell Erin and your folks we were talking hoops, okay? They don't need to know our secret.'

I nod. I'm a little uncomfortable with this secret, but when your coach gives you an assignment, you do it.

TWELVE

'So this Russ is going to walk with us *every day*?' Erin asks me.

We're sitting on her steps waiting for Boy21's grandparents to drop him off so we can walk to school and start our senior year.

'Looks that way,' I say.

'Why?' she asks.

I shrug.

I feel bad about keeping the secret from Erin, but Coach told me to keep Boy21's true identity hidden, so that's what I'm going to do. I know I can trust Erin. She's a great secret keeper. But for some reason, I also feel like I should let people make up their own minds about Boy21 – including Erin.

'You know Coach went to the Irish Pride Pub to talk with my brother,' Erin says.

I blink several times rapidly.

It surprises me to hear this, because **black** people generally don't go to the Irish Pride Pub, although Rod did play ball for Coach back in the day, so they know each other.

'Coach asked Rod to get the word out on the streets,' Erin says.

I raise my eyebrows. 'Really?'

'That Russ Washington is our friend.'

This means that Coach asked Rod for protection. If he did that, it means he also went to Terrell Patterson's older brother Mike. Mike Patterson controls much of the streets on the blacker side of town.

'Seems kind of strange for Coach to be sticking his neck out so far for a non-basketball player,' says Erin, fishing.

'Coach has a personal interest in Russ,' I say.

'Why's that?'

'They're sort of like family. Okay?'

'Okay,' Erin says, and then adds, 'so did you forget to tell me something?'

She gives me this funny look that makes me start to feel horny.

I cock my head to one side and squint at her.

She stands and spins around so that her new white back-to-school dress lifts a little and I can see her knees.

I just stare at her. She's probably the only girl in our entire school who'll be wearing a dress today. All the other girls will be wearing jeans or short shorts or tight miniskirts.

'How do I look, Finley?' she says.

I give her a smile, two thumbs up, and one raised eyebrow.

'Thank you,' she says. 'You look very handsome in your new Sixers T-shirt.'

Erin puts her hands on my knees and leans in for a kiss, but before our lips meet, I hear a car horn, and then Boy21 is getting out of a big old Cadillac.

We strap on our backpacks and meet him at the car.

Boy21's wearing a brand-new-looking outfit.

Tommy Hilfiger button-down shirt.

Dark blue jeans.

Nike Zoom Soldier sneakers.

His hair's been cut and shaved tight to his skull by a barber – no more nappy braids.

Instead of a backpack, he has a leather over-the-shoulder bag.

He looks sort of like a prep-school student, which will put him at a disadvantage in our school and make him stick out, because no one at our school has money, except drug dealers.

Erin offers her hand and says, 'I'm Erin. Nice to meet you.'

'Russ.' Boy21 shakes her hand without making eye contact.

'Where you from, Russ?' Erin asks.

'Out west,' he says.

This is when I realize that either the therapist has really healed Russell or Boy21 has gone incognito.

Out west?

It's such a true, grounded, not-weird answer.

I'm surprised by how disappointed I am.

'You'll look after our boy?' Mr Allen says from inside the Cadillac.

'Yes, sir,' I say.

'Thank you,' Mr Allen says, then smiles and looks me in the eye from under his old-style hat – the kind with a feather sticking out of the red band ringing the 360-degree short brim.

As we walk to school, Erin tries to engage Boy21 in conversation, but he only gives one- or two-word answers, asks Erin no questions, and kind of acts like I usually do, which makes me wonder if he's also a minimalist speaker in certain situations.

I keep waiting for her to ask this six-five kid the most obvious question, and, of course, she eventually does.

When she asks if Boy21 plays basketball, he says, 'No,' with conviction.

I'm ashamed to admit it, but I'm glad to hear he doesn't play basketball anymore. And I'm relieved that my spot on the team is secure.

She asks where exactly he's from out west – what town, what state?

He says, 'I forget.'

Erin gives me a worried glance, and then asks Boy21 if he likes Bellmont so far.

Russ shrugs.

'Was that your grandfather in the car?'

He nods.

'Do you live with him?'

'And my grams.'

'Where are your parents?'

'No more questions,' he says, then smiles awkwardly and adds, '*please*.'

Erin gives me another worried look.

When we turn onto Jackson Street, Erin says, 'There it is. Bellmont High.'

Our school is a long three-story brick building with a cop car perpetually parked out front. By the front doors are metal detectors manned by large grumpy people who perform random bag searches. Kids have tagged the outside bricks with all sorts of graffiti. In sloppy silver spray-paint cursive someone long ago wrote BELLMONT HIGH BLOWS HUGE COCK next to the gigantic silhouette of our mascot, which is a rooster. And those words are the first we read every morning.

The hallways are yellow and very loud. Girls laughing. People pushing one another. Lockers slamming. No one seems to notice Boy21, just like no one seems to notice us.

We squeeze through the crowds and check the lists posted in the hallway.

Boy21 is in my homeroom even though homerooms are arranged alphabetically and all the other *M* and *W* names are not grouped together.

This is when I realize that Coach has intervened. Our team has been so good for so long under Coach, he has a lot of power around here.

Boy21's locker is right next to mine and it just so happens that he's in every one of my classes and every single teacher has chosen to sit us together on the seating charts. This also means that Boy21's in all Advanced Placement classes, like me, which isn't saying much because our school isn't very academic. Don't think I'm smart. If you're polite and seem well behaved, you get placed in the AP classes.

To our teachers, Boy21's very respectful and formal, always maintaining eye contact.

He says nothing to the other students in the building. Even when they speak to him, he continues to look at the floor or the ceiling, not answering.

I worry that the other students will find him arrogant, which is not a good thing to be in our neighborhood, unless you like being beaten down.

During lunch, noticing his size and stature, the other

basketball players come over to my table, and Terrell says, 'Yo, White Rabbit, who dis?'

'This here is Russ Washington. He's new,' Erin says.

'You play sports?' Sir says. Sir is our starting small forward and our number one wide receiver. His mom named him Sir because she wanted people to show him respect. He's half Puerto Rican, which is a bit of a rarity around here.

Boy21 just shakes his head.

'Maybe you should try basketball,' Hakim says. He's our power forward. 'You're tall. You got the body for it.'

'I see you're in our AP English class. Who's your favorite author?' Wes asks. Like I said before, Wes is our center, and he's a bit of a bookworm. He's always reading books on the bus when our team travels. He wears a headlamp at night so he can keep on reading when it's dark out.

Boy21 doesn't look up or answer the question.

'Okay. I see how it is,' Terrell says. 'You a quiet one, just like your new friend here.'

'What's wrong with being quiet?' Erin asks.

'Nothing, White Rabbit's lil baby,' Terrell says.

I see the hurt look on Erin's face, but I don't say anything when she gets up and throws her trash away. I *wanted* to say something. Sometimes I really hate being a minimal speaker.

'Ladies and gentlemen!' Terrell yells with his hands above his head. 'Ladies and gentlemen!'

Everyone in the lunchroom stops talking.

When the room is hushed, Terrell says, 'Please welcome the new student. This here Black Rabbit, good friend to White Rabbit, and just as quiet. These people friends of mine too, understand? So just let them do rabbit things as they wish without paying them no mind. That's it. Enjoy your lunch.'

Some people laugh at Boy21's new nickname, but everyone understands that Terrell is officially putting Boy21 under his family's protection.

'Okay,' Terrell says. 'Now you rabbits do whatever rabbits do. And, White Rabbit, you get ready to rack up the assists this winter, you hear?'

'Sure thing.'

Terrell is wearing a huge diamond in each ear. Those are new. He never wore diamonds last year.

When my teammates leave, Erin returns to the table, but she won't look at me.

I know she wanted me to stick up for her when Terrell called her White Rabbit's lil baby, but I need Terrell to like me so that the basketball season will go well, which is my number one priority, and there are much worse nicknames that other girls in our school endure. This is why I'm looking forward to basketball so much. When it starts there will be plays to memorize and I'll be in the gym just about every night. The rest of the world will disappear.

When Boy21 finishes the sandwich his grandmother made him, he says, 'We are not rabbits.'

For the first time all day, Boy21 is looking into my eyes, and maybe it's me who's crazy, but it's like he's trying to communicate with me, sending messages through our pupils. The weirdest part is I think I sort of understand the message he's trying to convey.

When we leave the lunchroom, in the hallways, we're greeted by hundreds of references to rabbits.

'Yo, Black and White Rabbits!'

'What's up, Biggie Rabbit and Smalls Rabbit?'

'Carrots are comin'. We gon' feed dem rabbits!'

It's all playful teasing, especially since we are under Rod's and Mike's protection, but it gets kind of annoying nonetheless.

Neither Boy21 nor I say a word, and I have to admit that it feels good not being the only rabbit in the building.

THIRTEEN

Mr Gore's a tall, thin man with thick glasses and a Jheri curl hairstyle that the other students relentlessly make fun of. He's my guidance counselor, and I don't really like him, even though he smiles a lot, has a soft voice, and is always talking about looking out for my best interests.

He's pulled me out of English class on the first day of school, which seems unnecessary and makes me feel anxious because I had to leave Boy21 behind, and Coach won't like that.

Mr Gore's office is covered with bumper stickers – floor to ceiling. Each bumper sticker has the name of a college on it, which is sort of ironic, because not many of the students here will get to go.

'So,' Mr Gore says when I sit down, 'you thinking about your future at all?'

'Community college,' I say, because it's all I can afford without a scholarship, and my SAT scores are pretty mediocre. Dad says you can go to community college for two years and then transfer, which saves a lot of money in the end. I'll have to take out less in loans, which seems smart. And then I plan to follow Erin wherever she ends up playing basketball.

'You can do better,' Mr Gore says. 'But there will be time to discuss that later.' He leans forward in his chair. 'So tell me about the new kid, Russ Washington.'

'What do you want to know?'

'Oh, I don't know. Maybe why Coach asked you to shepherd him around school, for starters.' Mr Gore smiles and licks his lips. 'Why do you suppose he picked you?'

I shrug.

'I know about Russ's past, Finley. I'm in the inner circle, so to speak.'

He's evaluating me, trying to see what I know, or maybe he's trying to trick me into giving out information on Russ. I don't like the look on his face. It's almost like he enjoys messing with my mind.

'Tell me. Do you see any similarities between you and Russ?'

'We both play basketball,' I say, and then I wish I hadn't because I don't know if Mr Gore knew that already.

'True,' he says, which makes me feel better, 'but I'm thinking about something else. Something that maybe you need to talk about. Something you've kept bottled up for too long now.'

I know exactly what he means because he's been trying to get me to talk about this subject ever since I was a freshman, and it's really none of his business. He doesn't understand what he's messing with. Some things are definitely better left unsaid. Mr Gore doesn't live in this neighborhood, and it shows.

'Can I leave now?' I ask.

'I'm only trying to help you, Finley.'

'Coach told me not to leave Russ alone, so I have to get back to class.'

'You do everything Coach tells you to do without ever questioning his motives?'

'Yes.'

'Why?'

'He's my coach.'

'I'm worried about you, Finley. If you get to feeling like you're in over your head, you can always talk to me. I want you to know that. I'm a good lifeguard.'

Lifeguard?

Take a look around, Mr Gore. We're not exactly at the town pool.

I'm starting to get annoyed, and it must show,

because Mr Gore writes me a pass and holds it up between his fore- and middle fingers.

'You're free to go,' he says.

I bolt.

FOURTEEN

After the last bell of the day, Boy21 follows me to the gym, where I meet Erin for our after-school workout.

When I change into my workout clothes, I ask Boy21 if he'll be training with us, and he says, 'I just want to watch.'

I nod, and when I turn my head, I smile, because I don't want to help him earn my starting spot should he decide to come out for the team. I'm happy to let him sit on the sideline while I get stronger and faster. And as soon as I'm on the court sweating, feeling my heart race as my body moves, I stop thinking, sort of like I did when we were looking at sticker constellations, only more intense. Playing basketball makes everything else go away.

Russ sits in the bleachers while Erin and I shoot our patterns, practice free throws, and do our sprints. He sits in the football stadium while we dribble our five miles.

And he sits in the corner of the room while we lift weights. The whole time he watches us with this blank expression on his face.

Eventually, he begins doing his homework.

Boy21 waits on the sidewalk when I walk Erin up to her door and give her a kiss good-bye. And then he and I sit silently on my front steps until his grandfather comes to pick him up.

The next day his grandfather drops him off at Erin's house and he becomes my silent shadow once again.

FIFTEEN

Our physics teacher, Mr Jefferies, announces that we'll be taking a field trip to watch an IMAX Theatre film. It's about an expedition to fix some telescope in outer space called the Hubble.

'You won't believe how much of what we'll be talking about this year is applicable to space travel,' Mr Jefferies says while passing out the permission forms. 'You're going to see images that will absolutely blow your mind!'

My classmates seem happy about the field trip, mostly because it's something different and gets us out of school for half a day, but Boy21 doesn't even crack a smile, which is weird. I thought he'd be really excited to travel through space, even if it's only an IMAX movie.

In between classes, I say, 'You excited about the field trip?'

'Sure,' Russ says, but that's it.

I figure it's best not to bring up outer space too much,

so I just leave it alone. But whenever Mr Jefferies talks about the trip, Russ starts opening his mouth really wide and tapping his pen on his desk, which makes everyone stare at him. I wonder if that's his nervous tic.

On the day of the trip, as we're lining up outside the high school, I'm disappointed to see that Mr Gore is chaperoning along with Mr Jefferies. But I say hello to Mr Gore when he greets me.

Our class just fills the short bus that takes us to the Franklin Institute, which is in Center City, Philadelphia, only a half-hour drive away. This is only the second time I've ever been to Center City, and the first time I've been to the Franklin Institute. My dad's taken me to a few Sixers and Phillies games over the years, but those aren't in Center City.

Russ and I sit together on the bus. I look out the window the whole time, because I don't often get a chance to leave Bellmont. Before we get onto the highway, we roll through this one town called Robin Township, where everyone lives in a mansion. There's no trash on the streets, no graffiti on the trees, and shiny brand-new cars are everywhere. Some of the houses look as big as our school and the front lawns are longer and wider than football fields. It's like what you see on TV. I wonder what it's like to live in a town like that and if Boy21 had a big house out in California, but I don't ask him.

We drive through the city and down a street lined with

the flags of many different countries before we get out of the bus, climb a set of concrete stairs that lead to huge old-looking columns, and then into the Franklin Institute. While Mr Jefferies picks up our tickets, we wait next to a gigantic white statue of Ben Franklin in the biggest chair I have ever seen. There are several high-school physics classes here, and our classmates mingle with kids from other schools, but Boy21 and I just hang silently by Mr Franklin.

'You boys okay?' Mr Gore says.

I nod.

'Yep,' Russ says.

I notice that Russ is opening and closing his hands over and over again, like he's nervous or something.

Mr Jefferies huddles up our AP physics class, distributes the tickets, and says, 'When I was your age, I never dreamed I'd be able to experience what you are about to. Behold the modern wonders of science! Onward, young minds!' He's a complete dork. He's totally geeking out over the IMAX experience.

We follow him into the theater and take our seats.

It's like being inside a globe, because the round screen looks like the inside of an opened sky-blue parachute – making me feel as though I am somehow falling.

There's a general announcement about what to do if you feel nauseated. You're supposed to close your eyes or exit toward the back, but as we are in the middle of a long row, I figure it's pretty much impossible to escape. I hope the people behind me don't puke on my head. The movie begins shortly after the announcement ends.

It's an amazing experience, just like Mr Jefferies promised. Loud and vivid, and almost three-dimensional. It feels like we're floating through outer space and like we're really going to be part of the space mission. The speakers are so loud they make my rib cage vibrate. It looks like I could grab planets and stars as easily as picking leaves off a tree. And they even got Leonardo DiCaprio to narrate.

'This really is pretty amazing,' I whisper to Russ, but he doesn't answer – he has his hand over his mouth, like he's trying not to get sick.

When a picture of the space shuttle appears on the screen, Boy21 yells, 'I don't want to see this anymore!'

Several people make the *Shhh!* noise, and then Russ is out of his seat, climbing over people's knees, trying to escape the theater.

'Sit down!' someone yells through the darkness, but Russ keeps moving.

I stand and try to follow him, to make sure he's okay, because it's dark, the steps are steep, and Boy21 seems really upset, but Mr Gore says, 'Stay here, Finley!' and then he chases after Russ.

I figure Mr Gore will take care of the situation, so I return to my seat and try to get lost in the movie, but I can't.

Why did Boy21 get so upset?

The astronauts float around inside the space shuttle's cramped quarters, where there is no gravity. I watch them put on space suits and fix the Hubble Space Telescope. Some pictures of the cosmos are really truly amazing. It messes with my mind a little, seeing how much there is out there, how big everything is. Leonardo DiCaprio says there are billions of galaxies, each with billions of stars. Hard to imagine. From time to time, I wonder where Russ and Mr Gore might have gone and what they are talking about, but mostly I just watch the movie.

When the film is over, Mr Jefferies herds us all out of the Franklin Institute and we eat our bagged lunches under the huge columns on the steps, where we watch a fountain shoot into the air between the Philadelphia Free Library and some skyscrapers. When I'm halfway done with my tuna sandwich, I spot Boy21 and Mr Gore walking toward us. They cross the street and climb the steps. Our classmates are talking and laughing, so I'm really the only person who notices Russ's return.

'You okay now?' Mr Gore asks. His hand is on Russ's shoulder – like they're old friends.

Russ nods and sits down next to me.

Mr Gore walks toward Mr Jefferies, leaving me alone with Boy21, and the silence feels awkward – even to me. So I say, 'You missed a good movie. Stars look really different up close than they do from far away. And some of the clusters – it almost looked like some giant stuck his enormous finger into the universe and swirled everything up, or something. Does that sound weird?'

Russ looks at the cars passing by and doesn't answer me.

'Why did you leave?' I ask.

'I don't really want to talk about it, okay?'

'Sure.' I understand about wanting to keep quiet – I really do.

SIXTEEN

Late September is the first time the lunch ladies serve carrots. I wait for the dumping to begin, keeping my eyes on Terrell, but this other kid I don't know approaches first. He's looking sort of tiny in an oversize Eagles jersey, but he has this cocky look on his face. When we make eye contact he says, 'Time to feed the rabbits.' He tries to scrape a mushy orange mound onto my food, and Russ screams, 'WE ARE NOT RABBITS!' He's not frantic, like he was at the IMAX Theatre. He's just mad. He's intimidating, with a fierce look in his eyes and a wild edge to his voice. Not to mention his size.

The kid jumps back and drops his plate on the floor.

Everyone in the lunchroom turns and faces us.

Dead silence.

My eyes are wide open, and then I'm smiling. I don't need to worry about my new friend. He can take care of himself – and maybe me too.

No one tries to dump carrots on Boy21's or my food ever again.

Through the fall, Boy21's by my side every second of the day. Even on weekends, he comes to watch Erin and me practice, but he never once touches a basketball and he never really says anything of consequence to either of us.

He's just always there.

We take him to the mall and to the movies a few times. I wonder if something will set him off again and make him get all angry like he did about the carrot dumper, but his facial expressions never seem to change. He doesn't laugh when we laugh. He doesn't smile when we smile. He just sort of hovers around us, and since Erin and I are pretty easygoing people, we don't really mind, but we start to get curious.

Alone on my roof Erin asks me questions about Boy21, but I only shrug. I don't tell her what Coach revealed to me, which isn't much. I promised him I wouldn't and so I don't.

'Does he say anything interesting when I'm not around?' Erin asks.

'Not really,' I say. It's the truth, maybe because I never ask him any questions.

'What's wrong with him, do you think?'

'Some people are just quiet. Like me.'

She smiles. 'Quiet can be sexy.'

Suddenly Erin's lips are on mine and my mouth is

all hot and slippery. Then she pulls away again and says, 'I don't mind quiet, but Russ is always around. We're hardly ever alone anymore.'

'Does that bother you?'

'Yeah, a little. But at least he doesn't invade our roof time.'

We're kissing again. Hot sweetness.

After ten or so minutes of making out, my thoughts drift and I begin to wonder why Boy21 hasn't mentioned outer space since the first time we met, but I also figure it's probably best not to bring the subject up, because he's surviving his Bellmont experience nicely and I don't want to jinx that. Just surviving around here can be hard enough. Plus I don't want to trigger another IMAX Theatre-type experience.

I respect privacy.

Also, I like kissing Erin, so I decide to concentrate on the present moment.

SEVENTEEN

One night in late October, on my way home from Erin's, Boy21 pops out from behind a tree and says, 'Can we sit on your roof?'

It's late, but it's also Friday night, so I nod.

I'm no longer surprised to find Boy21 following me. It's just what he does. And like I said before, he gives Erin and me space when we need it.

We head to my house. He's carrying a white box tied with string, plus his over-the-shoulder bag. He looks a little fidgety and keeps opening his mouth extra-wide, as if he's stretching out his jaw or yawning like a lion, only he doesn't look tired at all.

My dad's putting on his jacket, getting ready to leave for work, when we go inside. He's wearing that resigned miserable face he dons whenever he thinks I'm not looking, or when he's just too tired to fake it. When he sees us, he says, 'Do your grandparents know you're here, Russ?'

'Yes, sir,' Boy21 says. 'My grandfather's coming to pick me up in an hour.'

'What's in the box?' Dad asks.

'Cupcakes,' Boy21 says.

'Seriously?'

Boy21 nods.

'Well, I'm off to work.'

Pop's passed out in his wheelchair again, dead to the world with a beer can in one hand, Grandmom's rosary beads wrapped around the other, and the TV remote in his lap. On the TV is an infomercial for some cleaning product endorsed by Magic Johnson, who keeps saying, 'This is just like me – *magic*!' every time the hostess wipes a stain off a couch or rug with the 'magic' wand cleaner.

'Wish I could watch the Lakers' greatest point guard of all time humiliate himself on a cable infomercial station, but somebody has to pay the bills around here, so heigh-ho! Off to work I go!'

Boy21 laughs at Dad's joke, which makes him smile and raise his hand. They exchange a dorky dad-type high five, and then Dad is gone.

'Be gone, old cleaning products!' Magic Johnson says as he shoots old bottles like basketballs into a faraway trash can. 'Magic is here. Magic! Watch out, stains! You don't stand a chance! Magic! Magic! Magic!'

Magic Johnson looks old.

'Let's go,' I say.

Boy21 follows me up to my bedroom.

I pop open the window and we climb out onto the roof. It's cool, but not too cold up here. Maybe like opening-a-refrigerator-door cool.

Once we're seated he opens the box and, surprisingly, a small package of birthday candles. The two cupcakes are store-bought. Because the light is still on in my room, I can see that someone has drawn space shuttles on the cupcakes with frosting. I start to worry because of Boy21's freak-out at the IMAX Theatre.

He sticks a candle deep into each cupcake so that the wicks stick out where the flames would exit each space shuttle.

He uses a lighter to ignite the wicks and then says, 'STS-120. T minus ten seconds. Eight seconds. T minus five. Four. Three. Two. One. And liftoff of *Discovery* – opening harmony to the heavens and opening new gateways for international science.'

Boy21 starts singing 'Happy Birthday.' His eyes look wild, crazy, manic.

'Happy birthday, dear Boy21. Happy birthday to you,' he sings, and then blows out the candles.

He hands me one of the cupcakes and says, 'I got you a vanilla and me chocolate,' and then takes a big bite out of his cupcake.

I wonder if the vanilla and chocolate comment was

a joke. He's not laughing, so I say, 'Happy birthday. If I had known—'

'One day short of completing my fifteenth trip around the sun, my father doesn't drive me to my high school,' Boy21 says in this really serious voice. 'In fact, we drive in the opposite direction. When I ask where we're going, he just smiles and laughs. We end up at the airport and when we check in, I realize we're headed to Florida. So I say, "Dad, are you delivering on your promise?" When he winks at me, my heart starts pounding, because I know exactly where we're going. We land in Florida and hit a hotel. He doesn't even have to confirm it for me, because I know we are about to fulfill his lifelong dream and mine.'

The wind blows and the few dry, brittle leaves still hanging on to the trees rattle. I shiver a little.

'The next day we drive to the viewing spot and I can see it – space shuttle *Discovery*. It stands huge on the tower, and only a small body of water separates us. We wait for what seems like forever for it to take off, wondering if there will be complications. But it takes off twenty minutes before noon and there is this awesome noise when the rockets are ignited – and then these massive clouds explode from the bottom of the ship and billow out forever and ever along the horizon and then it rises real slow . . . pushed upward by what looks like a bright cone of orange lava, and a long tower of clouds forms in its wake. It may have been the most beautiful thing I've ever seen. And I remember my father putting his arm around me as we stood and watched. When it was over neither of us said anything for a long time. We just stood there smiling. It was the best birthday I've ever had. The best day of my life.'

When Boy21 finishes his story, I don't know what to say. So this is why he freaked out on the physics field trip.

'Eat your cupcake,' he says.

I eat the whole thing in just a few bites. Vanilla. Rich. Moist. So sweet it makes my teeth ache.

We sit in silence for a long time.

'You want to see that launch?' Boy21 asks.

'How?'

'YouTube,' he says while pulling a laptop out of his bag. 'I downloaded it before I came.'

We watch the short video. Boy21 was quoting verbatim whoever was announcing the launch on the YouTube clip – all the talk about harmony for the heavens and gateways. I wonder how many times he's watched this video.

'Your dad,' I say. 'He was interested in outer space?'

'Fascinated by it. He used to read endless books. Was a big *Star Trek* fan. He loved the final frontier. We had several high-powered telescopes too. Still do, in storage out west.'

Boy21 looks into my eyes and I start to feel as though he's making a decision. It's weird. This is the most he's ever said about his past. I feel as though he's already let down his guard far more than he had intended. But then his facial expression changes and he's gone again, just like that.

'My father sent me a telepathic birthday card today. He says he has a present for me, but due to an unforeseen meteor shower in a galaxy that you Earthlings don't even know exists yet, he anticipates being a few Earth days later than he had originally planned, regarding the pickup. So it looks like you and I will be spending some more time together, Earthling known as Finley.'

Part of me wants to call him on the charade and put some direct questions to him, especially after all he's revealed tonight. He came here uninvited. He freely offered up the story about his father. He obviously wants to talk about all this stuff. But for some reason I don't ask him anything. Maybe it's just my nature to remain mute when I am unsure, which is always, but I feel like I should be asking questions – that conversation would help – and yet, I realize he's probably talking to me because I *don't* ask questions and just let him exist as he wishes to exist. I don't mind him being Boy21, but I sort of like Russell too.

Instead of talking we simply lie on our backs and look up at the sky, even though it's cloudy and we can't even see the moon.

When his grandfather pulls up to my house, Boy21 says, 'Thanks for eating cupcakes with me, Earthling.'

I walk him through my room, down the steps, and out the door.

Just before he gets into the car, Boy21 turns around and says, 'I wish you and I could travel through the cosmos together, Finley. You have that calming presence. Happy birthday to me – and thanks.'

'See ya, man,' I say, and then he's gone.

EIGHTEEN

I'm in my room trying to read *The Merchant of Venice* for English class, which is proving to be pretty hard, when something hits my bedroom window. The splat remains of a snowball are sliding down the glass. I open up the window and cold air rushes into my room just before I get blasted in the face with another snowball.

'Snowball fight!' Erin yells from across the street.

I throw on my jacket and shoes and race downstairs.

'Where's the fire?' Dad says as I pass him in the living room.

Erin drills me in the chest just as soon as I exit through the door.

The flakes are falling huge and fast and the whole neighborhood is coated in white. Something pretty magical happens whenever it snows around here. The neighborhood gets very quiet and all the trash, broken glass, and graffiti are hidden under the white, at least for a little while. It seems too early for snow, which makes this night even more beautiful – like an unexpected present.

While I scoop up some snow and pack it, Erin hits me three times, which is when I realize that she has stockpiled snowballs. Once I have one packed, I charge Erin and take aim. She ducks and I miss, so I decide to tackle her, but not too hard, because there isn't all that much snow on the ground. She doesn't put up much of a fight at first, but then she tries to wrestle me, so I grab her wrists and pin her arms with my elbows, and we kiss.

Our mouths are the warmest things in the world right now.

'Isn't it amazing?' she says as the snow falls past my ears and lands all around her head.

'It is.'

'Let's sit on the roof and watch it fall all night.'

'Okay.'

We see two headlights approaching, which seems weird because most people around here are afraid to drive in the snow.

We stand, and I recognize the Ford truck as Coach's.

'Why is Coach here?' Erin asks.

'Dunno.'

Coach pulls up slowly, rolls down his window, and says, 'Finley, take a ride around the block with me?'

I look at Erin and shrug.

'I'll go hit Pop with a snowball,' Erin says. She actually picks one up from her pile and then jogs to my home. I wonder if she'll really throw it at the old man, which she could get away with, because Pop loves Erin as much as I do.

I get into the truck and the heat streaming from the vents burns my fingers when I try to warm my hands.

Coach doesn't drive around the block. He says, 'How's Russ doing?'

'Fine.'

'Have you talked to him about playing basketball?'

'Yep,' I lie. Ever since his birthday he's been extra quiet, and I get the sense that he doesn't really want to talk about basketball or anything else, so I let him be. But Coach doesn't want to hear that.

'What does he say?'

'Nothing really.'

'Nothing?'

'No.'

'What does he say about basketball?'

'I don't think he wants to play basketball.'

'Russ said that, or you *think* it?'

'He's not really stable.'

'Are you a psychiatrist now, Finley?'

Coach has never talked to me like this before. There's sarcasm in his voice and I can tell he's annoyed with me, which makes me angry, because I have walked to school with Boy21 every day, eaten every school lunch with him, and allowed him to be my shadow for more than two months now. And tonight I was having a nice private moment with Erin before Coach interrupted us.

'No, sir,' I say.

'I expect you to make sure Russ gets his physical tomorrow after school in the nurse's office and that he shows up to the team meeting on Friday. Understood?'

'Yeah.'

'When you see the boy play, you'll understand why this is so important. Trust me.'

'Okay.'

Coach reaches through the darkness and squeezes my shoulder. 'Thank you, Finley. This is about more than basketball. More than the team. Russ likes you. You're helping him.'

I don't know what to say to that, because it sure doesn't seem like I'm helping Russ, and he really isn't getting better, as far as I can tell.

'Tell your family I said hello,' Coach says.

I nod and then run through the falling snow toward the house.

Erin's watching the Sixers game with Dad, and Pop's shirt is all wet, which lets me know that she really threw a snowball at the old man.

'This is one feisty broad,' Pop says to me.

Dad laughs. 'She ran in here and blasted Pop in the chest!'

'If I had legs . . .'

'Sure,' Erin says, 'the old no-legs excuse.'

There aren't many people who could get away with talking this way to Pop, but Erin's special to us. She's put her time in. She's family.

'Come on, Finley,' Erin says.

And then we're on the roof again, watching Bellmont turn white – one snowflake at a time.

'What did Coach want?' Erin asks.

'He thinks I should encourage Russ to play basketball,' I say.

'Cool,' Erin says as she climbs on top of me.

By morning almost all the snow has melted, so no snow day.

As we walk to school Erin says, 'Russ, you interested in playing basketball?'

'Don't know,' Russ says.

I glance at his face and he's sucking his lips in between his teeth. He catches my eye and it's almost like he's asking for permission. I know I'm supposed to encourage him to play, but for some reason I don't.

'Physicals are after school today in the nurse's office,' Erin says. 'Best get one just in case. You can go with Finley.'

Russ nods.

I don't say anything.

We both pass our physicals later that afternoon, but we don't talk about basketball.

On the day of the preseason meeting, Mr Allen calls to let us know that Russ will be out sick. This is the first day of school he has missed, and I wonder if it has anything to do with the meeting.

After school our team meets in the lunchroom and Coach quickly hands out permission forms and a practice schedule that begins the day after Thanksgiving. Just tucking the papers into my backpack gives me a rush, because this moment is the first official basketball experience of the year.

After the meeting, as my teammates hustle off to football practice, Coach says, 'Finley, can we talk?'

I stay behind and, once we're alone, Coach says, 'What's Russ been saying to you about basketball?'

This again? Why won't Coach lay off it?

'We got our physicals,' I say.

'That's good. But the boy refused to come to school today – the day of the basketball meeting. His grandparents told me he's talking about outer space again, saying his parents are coming to get him in a spaceship.'

I watch the janitor empty the trash cans on the other side of the cafeteria.

'Did you tell him that he should play ball? Have you been encouraging him, Finley?'

'He doesn't want to talk about basketball,' I say. 'We don't talk about much at all.'

Coach sighs and gets this disgusted look on his face. 'Listen. Just make sure he's at the first practice. Let's just see how he reacts to being part of the team, running drills, getting back to normal for him. He needs the routine. Even if he never plays in a game. Just being part of something can help. You, of all people, should know that.'

I have to admit, I'm getting a little pissed at Coach. Why isn't he hassling Terrell or Wes or any of the other starters, asking *them* to help Boy21? Why is this my mission alone? I just want to play basketball.

'I know you won't let me down,' Coach says, and then lightly slaps my right cheek twice.

NINETEEN

Thanksgiving Day has us wearing gloves, scarves, and hats.

Erin, Boy21, and I sip hot chocolate as we watch our football team lose their final game of the season on their home field.

People around here like football, but the atmosphere is underwhelming compared to the basketball games. It's Thanksgiving, so it's a little more lively than usual, but not much. Bellmont just isn't a football town.

Our marching band's halftime show's pretty awesome, though. They do a Michael Jackson tribute that ends with an amazing rendition of 'Thriller', complete with zombie dance moves.

Boy21 sits with us in the smaller, mostly white section of the stadium, which makes him stick out a little, but no one says anything.

It's not like our stadium is segregated intentionally,

but Bellmont citizens generally sit with the people they look most like, and that's the way it's always been.

The three of us cheer when our team does something good, but we don't say much else. The whole time I want to ask Boy21 if he'll be trying out for the basketball team tomorrow, but I also don't want to ask.

When Terrell throws a fourth-quarter interception, the Bellmont football team ends up finishing 2–6 for the season, so they don't make the playoffs. None of my basketball teammates were injured, so I consider football season to be a complete success and I know that Coach agrees.

As we exit the stands, we run into Mrs Patterson, Bellmont's number one basketball fan and Terrell's mother, who is wearing a leopard-print hat and a leather jacket that sort of looks like a bathrobe. She's very stylish. When she sees me, she yells, 'White Rabbit! Come on over here, boy.'

I walk over to Mrs Patterson and she gives me a big hug and then kisses both my cheeks. To her friends – who are all wearing Bellmont football jerseys over their coats and are the moms of non-basketball players – Mrs Patterson says, 'Did you know this here Pat McManus's boy? Time for the real season now. *Basketball!* This young man's gon' feed my son the rock all winter long and I'm gon' cheer White Rabbit and my Terrell on to the state championship. Ain't that right, White Rabbit?'

'Yes, ma'am.'

'Look how he quiet and respectful, just like his father was in high school,' a large woman with dark purple hair extensions says. All of the other women laugh and smile and say, 'Mmm-hmm!'

'Okay, White Rabbit,' Terrell's mom says, nodding a respectful but curt hello at Erin, who is standing with Boy21 ten feet away. 'You run off with your girlfriend and your tall silent shadow. Go on now.'

We find Coach hanging out with the other Bellmont faculty members in the parking lot drinking beer from paper cups and pretending that we students don't know what's in the cups. He tells me that he'll see me in the morning – which is when basketball season officially begins – wishes Erin luck, and then says he'll drive Boy21 home, because that's where he's having his Thanksgiving dinner, with the Allens.

Finally alone, Erin and I walk back to our neighborhood holding hands.

The few trees left around here have shed their leaves, but because no one in our neighborhood bothers to rake, we crunch our way down the sidewalks.

'You know,' Erin says, 'maybe we could stay together this basketball season. Maybe we don't have to break up?'

I don't say anything.

Erin and I have this conversation every year.

She argues that our schedules will keep us so busy that it won't even matter if we are together or not, but I believe that during basketball season, a romantic relationship is a distraction, and there's no way I can simply be friends with Erin. If I see her at lunch or before school or at my locker every day, I'll get horny, and I won't be able to focus one hundred percent on the season. I love Erin as much as I love basketball, which is a conflict of interest. And if we kiss on my roof or hold hands – these things will most definitely take my mind off my goals. With schoolwork and Pop to take care of already, I can't mentally afford to have a girlfriend during basketball season.

I love making out with Erin, and holding her hand, and the peachy smell of her hair after she showers – almost as much as I love the sweaty leather smell of a gym in winter, being part of a team, and working out with the guys. And while having a girlfriend and being on a team aren't mutually exclusive, both fill a need – maybe the same need. Basketball and Erin make the rest of the world go away – focus me, make me forget, and get the endorphins flowing. It's best to be addicted to one or the other. This will be the fourth season Erin and I have taken a break, and we've always gotten back together in the past, so why do I have this strange dreadful feeling tonight?

When it's clear that I'm not going to argue with her, Erin says, 'Don't you worry that I'll start dating someone else?'

I laugh because I know she's kidding.

Basketball will be her boyfriend for the winter, just like it'll be my girlfriend.

'So?' she says.

'You need to focus on *your* season too.'

She knows this is true because, deep down, Erin also wants to concentrate solely on basketball. She just gets a little needy the night before the season begins.

'Can't we at least walk to school together and talk? Sit together at lunch? Aren't you being a little extreme?' Erin's smile is playful. She's messing with me. I know she gets why we break for basketball.

'I have to stay focused,' I say. I think about the possibility of Boy21 actually playing, and then add, 'Especially this year.'

'Why?'

I shrug, because I'm not allowed to tell her the truth.

She gently elbows me in the ribs. 'Tell me why you said *this year*!'

I don't know what else to say.

'Why do you have to be so weird?' Erin says, but she squeezes my hand when she says it, so I know she isn't mad at me.

I decide to kiss her on the lips, and, because it's not officially basketball season yet, I do just that.

TWENTY

Erin and I eat our Thanksgiving meal at the Quinns'. The dining room is very narrow and it's hard to pull the folding chairs out so that you can sit down. None of the chairs match and the table is an old wood job with lots of scratches on it. The silverware is mismatched and crappy. Erin's parents are wearing depressing old sweat suits. Her mom's in a pink Minnie Mouse number and her dad's is plain navy blue.

Rod is there and I have to admit that he intimidates me, especially knowing what he allegedly did to Don Little.

During the meal, Rod says, 'Anyone in the neighborhood bothering you?'

'Nah,' I say. Rod's now got a tattoo on his neck. Something written in Irish, I think. I don't know Irish.

'What about you, Erin?' he asks.

'No,' she says. 'Do you ever play ball anymore, Rod?'

'Nope,' he says, which makes me sad because he played ball with us all the time when we were younger, and he was a great point guard. Dad used to take me to see him play back when Rod was at Bellmont High, playing for Coach. Rod was pretty awesome. I once saw him get a triple double against Pennsville – sixteen assists, eighteen points, ten rebounds.

'Your team going to be any good this year?' he asks me.

'I think so,' I say. 'Erin's team will be too.'

'Coach is pretty much the only good black man I've ever met,' Rod says, ignoring my comment about his sister. 'And that's really sayin' something.'

Erin opens her mouth, no doubt to call Rod on his racist statement, but then she thinks better of it. She doesn't want the family to fight on Thanksgiving, especially since Rod hardly visits anymore, which bothers Erin. She misses Rod – the *old* Rod who used to play ball with us when we were kids. He never used to say racist stuff.

I think about saying something too, like *I know a lot of good black men*, but I also know my place in the neighborhood. Truth is, I'm afraid of the new tattooed Irish mob Rod, just like everyone else.

We eat in silence for a few minutes.

Erin's parents are older than my father and a little strange too. Her dad's quiet like me and avoids eye contact during the meal. Her mother's a nervous woman who makes so many trips to and from the kitchen that she never really sits down long enough to eat, let alone have a conversation.

Erin's parents look a little like wrinkly deflated zombies. Sounds funny to say, but it's true. There's not a lot of life in either of them.

In some ways, their row home is a little nicer than mine. They even have a flat-screen TV, a computer, and Internet access, but I wonder how much of that Rod covers, especially since Mr Quinn has been out of work for a long time and Mrs Quinn works down at the town hall as a secretary, so she can't make all that much cash. There are some questions you simply don't ask in Bellmont, because no one wants to know the answers.

'I'll get you some more meat' is the most Mrs Quinn says to me during the meal.

Erin tries to get everyone talking by asking what each of us is thankful for.

'Turkey,' her father says.

'Family,' her mom says.

'Guinness and Jameson,' Rod says.

'Basketball,' I say.

'Finley,' Erin says.

'And Erin,' I say.

'And basketball,' Erin says.

Erin and I look each other in the eyes.

Rod snorts and shakes his head.

We finish eating in silence.

Just as soon as he swallows his last bite of pumpkin pie, Rod leaves.

Mr and Mrs Quinn both fall asleep on the couch.

After Erin and I wash and dry the dishes, we go to my house, where we find Pop passed-out drunk in his wheelchair again, clutching Grandmom's green rosary beads, just like every other holiday, because special occasions make him miss his wife even more.

We present my dad with the plate of food that Erin wrapped up and sit with him while he eats.

'What are you thankful for?' Erin asks Dad.

'That my son has such a good friend,' Dad says. 'And for this plate of delicious food too.'

Erin smiles.

'You two ready for basketball season?' Dad asks.

'You know it,' Erin says.

'Man, I wish I was still playing high-school basketball,' he says. Dad gets this sad faraway look in his eyes, probably because he was dating Mom back then.

No one says anything and Dad finishes eating.

Once his slice of pie is gone, Erin and I go up to my bedroom and climb out onto the roof. We bring my comforter with us, wrap ourselves up into a giant cocoon, and breathe in the crisp fall air, which makes me think of opened refrigerators again.

I had planned to make out with Erin for a half hour straight, because this is the last time we'll kiss for at least three months. If either of our teams goes deep into the playoffs, it could be four months before I taste Erin's lips again, so as I run my hands between her shirt and her smooth, strong back, I try to focus on being with my girlfriend tonight and put basketball out of my mind, but I can't.

'What's wrong?' Erin finally says. 'You're not into this at all.'

'I'm nervous about tomorrow,' I say.

The wind blows hard and I shiver, even though Erin is on top of me now and her body is very warm.

'Why?' she asks. 'You've been the starting point guard for two seasons now. Coach loves you. You're in the best shape of your life, and you've worked so hard in this off-season. You've done everything you possibly could to prepare. It's going to be a great year for you. Hard work yields big-time rewards, right? Remember our summer motto.'

When I don't say anything, Erin says, 'What's going on with you? You've been weird for a couple of weeks now. You better tell me now before we break up at midnight or this is going to eat you up for months.'

'Can you keep a secret?' I ask her, because she's right: I need to talk about this. I know I'm betraying Coach by telling Erin, and I feel guilty about that, but I just can't keep it in any longer.

'You know I can.'

I stare into her shamrock-green eyes and then, before I can stop myself, I say, 'Russ's parents were murdered.'

'What?'

'He's here because his parents were murdered and then he went crazy and had to live in a home for kids with post-traumatic stress. Whenever we're alone, Russ calls himself Boy21. He says he's from outer space and that his parents are going to come and pick him up in a spaceship.'

Erin's mouth opens, but she doesn't say anything.

'I'm serious. When he came to live with his grand-parents, Coach told me everything and asked me to help Russ. Coach was good friends with Russ's dad. Russ is using a fake last name, because he's a nationally recruited point guard who used to play in California. Coach wanted me to help Russ assimilate to Bellmont so that he could play ball for us. He's going to take my position, Erin. I haven't said anything before about this because Coach asked me not to tell anyone.'

'Wow,' Erin says. 'I mean, *wow*! That explains a lot. He really believes he's from outer space?'

'I think it might just be an act, but he talks about it all the time.'

'He has an athlete's body. Anyone could see that,' Erin says. 'Why didn't you tell me about this before?'

'Coach asked me not to,' I say.

'You should've told me. I tell you *everything*. We both know secrets keep people stuck here in Bellmont forever. Do you want to get stuck in Bellmont forever? Or do you want to leave with me?'

'You know I want to be with you. I definitely want to leave this neighborhood.'

'Well then?'

Erin seems really pissed, so I say, 'I'm sorry. Okay?'

I look up at the sky. There're too many clouds to see anything.

She's right about secrets, but Erin knows I do everything Coach tells me to do.

When I feel like the tension's gone, I say, 'I don't want Russ to take my position.'

'Maybe Coach was just exaggerating? Maybe Russ isn't that good?'

'I don't know. That's the problem. I wish I knew so I could wrap my mind around it.'

Erin kisses the end of my nose. 'You don't even know if Russ is going to show up tomorrow. Right?'

'It doesn't seem like he really wants to play ball.'

'If he does show, he hasn't practiced in a long time. He's not in game shape, so you have the advantage there. Coach would never forget about you – about all the hard work you've done for the team, and what you've done for Russ too. Coach asked you to be Russ's friend, and you did exactly that – for Coach. And let's say, just for the sake of argument, that your worst fear comes true. Even if you lose your starting position – worst-case scenario – Coach will use you as the sixth man, right?'

'I don't want to be the sixth man,' I say. 'I want to be the starting point guard and team captain.'

'Like I said before – play hard tomorrow. Your game's the only thing you can control.'

I kiss her cheek and she wiggles her body down so that she can rest her head on my chest.

'Russ's parents were really murdered?' Erin asks me.

'Yes.'

'That unfortunately explains why he's so quiet. I mean, my God. *Murdered.*' Erin pauses, and then says, 'Is that why Coach picked you to help Russ?'

'What do you mean?'

'I don't know. I just thought that – well—'

'What?' I ask.

'Forget it,' Erin says.

'I'm sorry I didn't tell you earlier, but Coach—'

'How did it happen?'

'How did *what* happen?'

'How were Russell's parents murdered?'

'I don't know,' I say. 'He doesn't like to talk about it. I can tell.'

'He doesn't like to talk about *anything*,' Erin says.

'I can understand why,' I say, and that seems to end the conversation.

We lie there breathing together for a bit, and I can see my breath in the moonlight.

I feel my heart beating so close to hers.

Erin says, 'You do realize that Russ really enjoys being around you? He follows you around all day like a lost puppy. And the way he looks at you. You don't see it, do you? He likes you. He needs you. You've been a good friend to him this year. You've been helping him. If he comes out for the team, it'll probably just be so that he can continue to shadow you this winter. So that you two can continue to hang out.'

'He only follows me because Coach told him to,' I say. 'That's the only reason.'

'No, it's not, Finley. It's because you're a good person. It's because you're easy to be around. It's because you are *you*. You don't put demands on people and you never say anything negative – ever. So many people suck the life out of everyone they're around, but you don't do that. You give people strength just by being you.'

I don't think Erin is right, but I don't say anything about that.

We lie on the roof holding each other until midnight.

We kiss once more on her front steps, after I walk her home.

'Good luck this season,' I say.

'You'll be great this year,' she says.

'Okay.' I take a step back.

'Do we really have to break up?'

'Just for a few months.'

'Will you be my boyfriend again once basketball season is over?' she asks.

I nod, even though it breaks the rules. In past years I've argued that we have to break up for real and that taking a leave of absence from our relationship is not the same as breaking up, because we'd just be thinking about the day when we'll be reunited, which would distract us from basketball. But the truth is we both know this will really only be a temporary separation. We're definitely going to spend the rest of our lives together.

'I better go. We need to sleep, rest up for day one,' I say.

She nods once and then goes inside.

I'm a single man.

I'm simply a basketball player – a point guard.

And it's going to be an interesting season, for sure.

THE SEASON

'Sometimes a player's greatest challenge is coming to grips with his role on the team.'

Scottie Pippen

TWENTY-ONE

Just like every other year, I'm the first one to arrive.

We have the early practice today, so the gym hasn't been opened up yet. I have to wait outside for Coach to show.

It's cold, especially since I'm wearing shorts.

The six-seven Wes Reese walks up with his nose in a book that's covered in brown paper. He tries the door without even seeing me. When he finds it locked he looks up from his book and says, 'Hey there, White Rabbit. Didn't see you.'

'Yo,' I say.

He holds his book up. 'Ralph Ellison. *Invisible Man*. Good stuff.'

I nod even though I've never read Ralph Ellison, and, truthfully, I don't know who he is.

Sir and Hakim show up next and we all slap hands.

More and more players begin to arrive, but no Coach.

Terrell gets dropped off by his brother Mike, who's driving a pimped BMW with chromed-out rims and tinted windows. The bass from his stereo hits my chest as he cruises away.

'Where Coach?' Terrell asks.

'Dunno,' I say.

He's wearing a gold chain with his number dangling from it – 3. That's new, I think.

Assistant Coach Watts shows up and we know Coach is officially late, because our JV coach is never on time.

Coach is never late.

Never.

What's up?

Suddenly, as I stand there huddling with the other players, I realize why Coach is late.

I break out in a cold sweat.

He's trying to talk Boy21 into coming to practice.

'White Rabbit, why you look so nervous?' Terrell asks me.

I shake my head and shrug.

'You should open your damn mouth more,' Hakim says to me. 'The only time I hear you speak is when you calling out plays.'

'What you reading?' Terrell says to Wes.

'Ralph Ellison,' Wes says without looking up.

'Who Ralph Ellison?' Terrell asks.

'One of the most important African American writers,'

says Wes, sounding like what some people would call *bougie*. 'Part of your heritage. An author you should really read.'

Terrell flashes the rest of us a funny expression and then grabs the book out of Wes's hands.

'Give that back to me!' Wes says.

Terrell inspects the book and then yells, '*Harry Potter*! This fool's readin' 'bout a boy wizard!'

Everyone laughs at Wes, even Coach Watts, but I'm not really sure why.

So what if Wes wants to read *Harry Potter*?

Who cares?

I want to say something to Terrell, but my tongue won't work and I feel my face turning red.

'We have to read it for Advanced Placement English,' Wes says. 'It's assigned reading. It's not my fault!'

'That true, White Rabbit?' Sir asks me.

'Absolutely,' I say, just to save Wes from sounding like a liar, and he shoots me a thankful look before he grabs his Harry Potter book back from Terrell.

'Any black people in Harry Potter books?' Terrell asks.

'Why does that even matter?' Wes says.

Before Terrell can answer, Coach pulls up in his truck with Boy21.

'Look who it is, White Rabbit,' Terrell says. 'It's your shadow. Thought Black Rabbit didn't play basketball?'

'Why's he ridin' with Coach?' Hakim asks.

'Dunno.' I peer up into the sky. Gray everywhere.

Coach unlocks the gym door and we all go inside.

I decide to ignore Boy21 and simply focus on my own goals. If I don't even talk to Erin during basketball season, and Erin's been my best friend since elementary school, then I shouldn't feel bad about ignoring Boy21. Time to prioritize. Time to play basketball. My teammates need me.

Right?

The only problem is that Boy21's parents were murdered and I know that I should be helping him, because he's suffering.

As we shoot around, Boy21 hovers near me, but I just keep moving – chasing rebounds. I never really minded having a shadow, but Boy21's presence feels heavy now, like it could slow me down. It's almost like having a girlfriend during the season – an extra worry.

I catch Russ's eye once and he looks really nervous, scared, which makes me angry because, if Coach's assessment is right, Boy21's the best basketball player in the gym, so what does he have to worry about?

When Coach blows the whistle we all sit against the wall. Boy21 plops down next to me, but I don't look at him. Coach says he only has enough uniforms to keep eighteen players, and cuts will be next week. There are twenty-six players sitting against the wall, which means eight players will not make the team.

Coach talks about our goal of winning a state championship. He talks about teamwork and hard work and how we're going to become a unit – a family. He says all the stuff he says every year.

I've heard these words a thousand times before, but even so, Coach's message makes me feel lighter, focused. My muscles are ready. My heart wants to beat hard. My mind wants to shut off. It's like falling into a trance.

The season is the only thing that really makes any sense in my life. There's a clear objective. People come together to accomplish this objective, and the community celebrates that. Basketball's the only thing around here that gets done right, the only thing that people consistently support. It's the best thing in my life by far, except for maybe Erin.

Soon we're running full-court drills, but I can't even lose track of Boy21 in the shuffle of the lines because he's performing so horrifically that everyone notices him.

The first pass he makes goes into the stands.

The first four shots he takes are air balls or bricks.

He gets beat every time while playing defense.

He looks awful – like he's drunk or something.

His shoulders are slumped forward and his knees are together, which is a terrible basketball stance. He's always looking up at the lights, like he's expecting to be beamed up into outer space or something, or maybe like he's praying. It's clear that he really doesn't want to be here.

But the funny thing is: I'm not happy about this. I actually start to worry about Boy21, because the expression on his face makes it looks like he's about to cry. I worry so much about Boy21 that it starts to affect *my* game, and when I throw a bad pass, Coach yells, 'What's wrong with you, Finley? You're competing for your starting spot too! No free rides!'

Coach has never yelled at me like that before. It makes me really nervous and confused.

In order for Coach to be happy with my performance, both Boy21 and I need to play well, which seems unfair. I'm connected to Russ in a way that the other players are not.

When Coach goes over the new offensive plays, I'm relieved to find myself still practicing with the first squad.

Boy21 runs with the second team, but he can't seem to remember the plays, even after watching me run them for a good twenty minutes.

He's awful.

Too awful.

Unbelievably terrible.

It's almost comical.

The other starters exchange angry looks and shake their heads and mumble curse words, because Russ is single-handedly ruining the flow of practice.

It's like Boy21 has never touched a basketball in his life.

It's almost like he's intentionally –

That's when I understand what's going on. Why Coach looks so frustrated and angry.

For the next two hours I play as hard as I can, but my mind's elsewhere.

Toward the end of practice the girls' team enters the gym. I glance up at Erin. She's watching my every move, rooting for me with her eyes and fighting an urge to wave. I wish I could tell her what's going on, but we won't be speaking for another three months, and that's just that.

My practice uniform is heavy with sweat. My hair and skin are slick. My muscles are tired and so is my mind, because of Boy21. Basketball has never been so stressful before. I'm thinking too much. It's better when athletes don't think.

As we run our end-of-practice sprints I make sure that I finish first every time, even though Sir, Hakim, Terrell, and probably Boy21 are much faster than I am when they're not tired. I'm tired too, but because I'm not as gifted as the other top players, I have to outwork talent, like Dad says, so I push myself harder and win every sprint by five to ten feet.

I try to make up for my poor practice and soon my lungs are aflame and my legs are screaming, threatening to quit on me.

Each time, Boy21 finishes dead last.

He looks pathetic.

'Bring it in,' Coach says.

We huddle together and put our hands in the center so that we make a big wheel of bodies with arm spokes.

Coach says, 'Second session starts at three. Finley and Russ, I'll see you in the coaches' office. On three, team! One, two, three—'

'Team!' everyone yells, and then I follow Coach into his office and Russ follows me. Coach Watts herds everyone else into the locker room and the girls take the court with the noise of a dozen or so basketballs being dribbled and twice as many pairs of sneakers pounding the hardwood floor.

Boy21 and I stand on opposite sides of the office.

Coach shuts the door and says, 'Finley, I asked you to help Russ transition to Bellmont, correct?'

I nod.

'Based on what I told you about Russ, do you not think that our team would have a better chance of achieving its goals if he played for us this year?'

Boy21 looks at his shoes.

'He's known that you were clued in from the start, because I told him about our conversations,' Coach says. 'So just answer my question, Finley.'

'Yes.'

Yes, the team would be better with a nationally recruited all-star point guard playing instead of me.

'Then why did you tell Russ not to come out for the team?' Coach asks.

My eyes almost pop out of my head. I never told Boy21 not to come out for the team. *Never!* I open my mouth but no words will come. My tongue just won't work.

It feels like my heart is a squirrel trying to climb up and out of my throat. My hands are balled up. Sweat beads are jumping from my face to the floor.

'He never exactly *said* that to me,' Boy21 says. 'Not with words.'

'What?' Coach says to Boy21. 'You told me this morning that Finley said you shouldn't play for our team.'

'That's not what I said,' Boy21 says. 'I said I could tell he didn't want me to play. He never told me not to, but he never asked me to play either – he never encouraged me, and I could just tell. Coach, this is Finley's senior year. I don't want to come in and ruin it for him.'

'We do what's best for *the team*,' Coach says. 'Remember what we've been talking about?'

'Coach, Finley's been so cool to me. He's a good person. He loves this game a lot more than I do. He worked so hard in the off-season. Much harder than I worked. I can't just jump in and take his starting spot. What kind of friend would I be?'

I study Boy21's face for a long moment.

He doesn't crack a smile.

He doesn't even blink.

He's completely sincere.

He wasn't going to play basketball this year just so I could start. That's why he was pretending he couldn't play during practice – just for my benefit. I feel something akin to what I feel for my own family, Erin, and Coach as I realize what's going through Boy21's mind. I'm not sure anyone has ever offered to make such a sacrifice for me.

'I can't take his number either. It wouldn't be right,' Boy21 says.

I look down at the number 21 on my practice jersey, the number I've been wearing since freshman year. I knew this was coming, but I feel differently than I thought I would. Of course he'd want to wear that number.

'Finley, you never told Russ not to play basketball?' Coach asks.

'No, sir,' I say.

'I owe you an apology, then.'

I don't really want an apology, but I'm feeling relieved. I just want to play basketball. I just want Coach to be happy with me.

'It's been a strange situation for all of us. Listen. How about this? I'm going to step out of the room for a few minutes and see if you two can work something out,' Coach says, and then he does just that.

Boy21 and I stand in silence for what seems like a long time.

I can hear the squeaking of sneakers on the court and the girls' coach yelling about hard work. The office smells of sweat and leather – like an old baseball glove. It's pretty dusty too.

I'm sort of pissed about being put in this position. Isn't it Coach's job to make sure everyone's on the same page? And he just leaves the room?

Eventually Boy21 says, 'I don't want to ruin your senior season, Finley. I don't even care about basketball anymore.'

I don't know what to say, so I say nothing.

Coach yelling at me during practice messed with my head, and I still feel a little out of sorts, even though I realize Boy21 basically lied to him. But I'm not mad at Boy21 at all. I've never met anyone who would cease doing what they are best at just so I could do it. I don't think I'd stop playing basketball for *anyone*.

'And I can't play unless I'm number twenty-one. I have to be twenty-one. That's just the way it is,' he says.

'Why?' I ask.

'My father was number twenty-one in high school, and he's monitoring me from outer space. I promised I'd always wear number twenty-one for him, so long as I played ball. And now that he's on a spaceship so far away,

I feel like it's more important than ever – but if I don't play basketball this year, I won't have to worry about numbers at all. Which is good, because you're already number twenty-one, and you're my best Earthling friend. I could just root for you from the stands, which could be a lot of fun. I could sit with your dad and Pop and we could cheer you on until I leave this planet. And I think Mom and Dad will be coming soon to take me into outer space, so what's the point of me playing basketball anyway?'

I look into Russell's eyes. He's fighting back tears. I wonder if he really thinks his parents are on a spaceship or if he's just using space as some sort of shield – as a layer of words that allows him to express himself honestly almost in camouflage, as strange as that sounds.

Something is going on. It's like Boy21's giving me clues by making up stories about outer space.

Why?

This is the first I've heard Russ talk about outer space since we watched the space shuttle launch on my roof to mark his birthday.

If he's as good as Coach says he is, I know what's best for the team, and I've always put myself second for the team. That's what good basketball players do.

I think I know what's best for Russell.

I think about what good friends do.

I take off my number 21 practice jersey and toss it to Boy21.

He catches it and says, 'Finley, if I take this, if I start to play basketball to the best of my abilities – especially if I use my extraterrestrial powers – there's no way that you can beat me out for the position of point guard. You'll have absolutely no shot.'

'We'll see about that,' I say.

'You have to promise me that you'll be my friend regardless. I need you to be my friend. Please promise me.'

'I'm your friend no matter what happens.' I mean it.

'I'll hold back for as long as I can, but eventually, I won't be able to control myself,' he says. 'When I play basketball, something inside of me changes. It's just the way I'm programmed.'

'I don't want you to hold back.' If he's going to take my spot, he at least owes it to me not to hold back. I want to win or lose it fair and square.

When Boy21 doesn't say anything in response, I say, 'Do you really believe that your parents are coming in a spaceship to take you away?'

'Yes. Early in the new year, most likely, but it's hard to tell because Mom and Dad are not using Earthling calendars anymore, since they no longer reside in this solar system. Your calendar is based solely on the Earth's rotation around the sun. Once you pass Pluto, your Earth calendars are meaningless.'

'But you're still not going to talk about outer space with our teammates, right?'

'They'll know I'm not human when they see me play basketball,' he says. 'I won't be able to keep it a secret, because my skills are . . . *otherworldly*.'

I nod slowly, waiting for Boy21 to start laughing, for Coach to come running in with the rest of the team, pointing at me and howling at the elaborate practical joke, but that doesn't happen.

These words coming out of any other boy's mouth would sound like hyperbole or plain old trash talk, but Boy21 is dead serious. It's not even like he's proud of his skills. He's willing to hide his ability as if it were something to be ashamed of.

'You believe me, right, Finley? You believe I'm going back up into the cosmos with my parents. You of all people,' he says.

I nod. 'Do you mind if I talk to Coach alone?'

'Okay.'

He leaves and Coach shuts the door behind him.

'I'm sorry I doubted you, Finley,' Coach says. 'The situation has been hard on me. His father was a good friend of mine, so I feel a certain sense of—'

When Coach doesn't finish his sentence, I swallow once and wait.

Coach says, 'You gave Russ your number?'

I nod.

'You're a good kid, Finley. *A real good kid.* I'm making you and Terrell captains. I wasn't going to tell you until later, but considering the circumstances, I—'

'Coach, he really believes his parents are coming for him in a spaceship.'

'I'm not so sure about that.'

'He needs help.'

'He's getting it. Russ sees a psychologist twice a week. You want to know what Russ told his grandparents two weeks ago?'

I don't think Coach should be telling me what Boy21 says to his grandparents in confidence, but he keeps talking.

'Russ said his parents were going to pick him up in October – in their spaceship – but he sent a message using his mind or something like that. He asked his parents if he could stay on Earth for a few more weeks because he'd made a friend named Finley and Finley has a "calming presence." He said he was enjoying your company.'

I swallow again.

'He's on the edge, Finley. I don't think I have to tell you what that means, because you're a smart kid. When you see him play – really play ball – everything will make sense to you. Trust me on this one.'

When I leave the coaches' office the rest of my squad is long gone. The second-string girls' team is going over a zone defense, so Erin's back is against the wall; she's hugging her legs and resting her chin on her knees. Her eyes are on me, which is when I realize I'm shirtless. I see concern on her face, but I can't think about Erin now so I just turn my head and go change in the locker room.

I find Boy21 outside and he follows me to the town library.

In the young-adult section two copies of *Harry Potter and the Sorcerer's Stone* are available, so I check out both and hand a copy to Boy21.

'Wes was taking heat for reading this. He told Terrell it was required reading for AP English,' I explain.

Boy21 nods.

Wes is our teammate, so we get his back.

Boy21 follows me home, where I make sandwiches and we eat with Pop, who is sober enough to mind his manners and ask us questions about practice, all of which I answer vaguely, and then Boy21 and I hang in my room and read *Harry Potter* until it's time to go back to the gym.

The book's about a kid who has an awful life but gets a chance to escape it when he finds out his dead parents were wizards. Reading it makes me wonder if I'll ever escape Bellmont, and, if so, what sort of life I might have somewhere else.

We arrive to the second session early so we continue to read in the bleachers while the girls finish practicing.

Wes sits down next to us, notices what we're reading, and then whispers, 'You guys don't have to do this.'

I can tell he's touched by the way he's looking at me, so I give him a smile. I hold up my fist and he gives me a pound.

'It's a really good book,' Wes says, and then pulls out his copy. 'Surprisingly good.'

When Terrell, Hakim, and Sir see us reading *Harry Potter* they just shake their heads.

During the second session Boy21 picks up his game, but not too much. I actually think he plays just well enough to make the team, but not well enough to challenge me for my position.

My ego wonders if all his and Coach's talk about how good he is might just be inflated hype, but there's something deep down inside me that knows Boy21's still holding back.

He's not going one hundred percent and doesn't get physical with anyone.

He's simply coasting without making any mistakes.

He's *in* the game, but he's not *playing* the game.

After she changes in the locker room, Erin sits alone

in the stands for a while watching us, but then halfway through practice I look up and she's gone.

I don't like her watching me practice because it makes me nervous, but I already miss her.

TWENTY-TWO

We practice, we go to school, we do our homework, we read *Harry Potter* . . . and that's really all Boy21 and I do.

When he asks why we don't see Erin anymore, I say, 'Basketball is my girlfriend now,' which makes him laugh, and I guess it does sound pretty funny.

We finish reading the first Harry Potter book a few days after Wes does.

Before Friday-afternoon practice, while shooting around in the gym, Wes says, 'So what did you think of *Sorcerer's Stone*?'

'If one of your friends had magical powers,' Boy21 says, 'would you want to know about it?'

'Like Harry does?' Wes says, moving his shoulders back six inches and scrunching up his face. '*Real* magical powers?'

'Powers that not everyone else has,' Boy21 says.

'Hell yes, I'd want to know,' Wes says.

'What if it meant you'd never see them again? Not everyone gets to go to Hogwarts, right?' Boy21 starts rubbing his palms against his sides.

'Why you askin' me this, Russ?'

Boy21 rolls the back of his head across his shoulders.

Wes cocks his head sideways at me, but I only shrug.

'You guys want to come over my house tonight and watch the movie version of the book?' Wes asks. 'My mom got it for me on Netflix.'

So that night the three of us watch the movie version of the book, which is pretty good. Lots of magic, castlelike buildings, and friendship.

After the movie Wes takes us into his room and plays his favorite rap group, N.E.R.D. The music is very funky, not like the straight-up gangsta rap music I usually hear in the neighborhood, although there *is* a lot of cursing.

(I don't really listen to music much, maybe because I have no iPod. Music is okay, but I don't go crazy for any one type.)

'Do you guys know what N.E.R.D. stands for?' Wes asks.

'What?' I say.

Boy21 says, 'No one. Ever. Really. Dies.'

'You a fan, Russ?' Wes says.

Boy21 nods and smiles.

'You seen the Seeing Sounds Game on their website?' Wes says. 'Retro. *Badass futuristic funky.*'

Wes punches up the N.E.R.D. website on his computer and then hits the right link. The Seeing Sounds Game has an outer-space theme.

No wonder Boy21 likes this group.

A giant gorilla chases the group members across a moonlike landscape.

'It's an old-school video game. You play as one of the group members,' Wes says, and then he and Boy21 take turns playing.

When they finish messing around on the N.E.R.D. website, Wes suggests we form a Harry Potter book club. He wants to read each book and watch each film in between readings. I always thought that book clubs were for rich women, but it feels good to be included in something other than basketball.

We both agree to join him and pick up copies of *Harry Potter and the Chamber of Secrets.*

I like Wes. We've always been friendly, but I'm starting to feel like maybe he could be a real friend to both Boy21 and me – someone we hang out with regularly. Maybe because he's the weird type of kid who forms a Harry Potter book club. Wes is strange like that. Odd like us.

Why didn't I hang out with Wes before?

As we walk back to the Allens' home, I ask Boy21 about N.E.R.D. and the outer-space theme of their website, and he says, 'That's just pretend outer space, not real outer space, but it's true that no one ever really dies.'

I raise my eyebrows when he glances at me.

'Matter cannot be destroyed nor created,' he says. 'That's one of the basic principles of the universe, first of all. But then there is your life force, which is contained and trapped here on Earth by your body – your flesh – which is like a prison. When you Earthlings die, your life force is released and then you're free to travel through the galaxies again. That's not death, it's liberation.'

'Umm . . . *what?*' I say.

'I only tell you, Finley, because you seem to be enlightened. The rest can't handle such ideas.'

I feel a little proud knowing that Boy21 thinks I'm special, but I also feel a little sad too, because Boy21 is suffering. Deep inside his brain there is a war going on – a war that he's losing.

There's not much I can do to help him.

TWENTY-THREE

I see Erin in the halls of our school and in the gym. We pass and she always tries to catch my eye or rub elbows, pretending it's an accident, but I keep walking with my eyes straight ahead, like I don't notice her.

Coach names Terrell and me this year's captains during a team meeting. The team celebrates by eating a dozen or so pizzas.

The day before our first game, Coach announces the starting lineup, and I get the nod at point guard.

All is going as planned, and I sort of forget about Boy21's ability to take away my starting position.

I'm playing organized basketball again.

On the court it's all adrenaline and sweat and movement and leather and cheering and squeaking sneakers and high fives and the feeling that I can and am accomplishing something.

Off the court it's all anticipation, hunger, counting

down the minutes until the next practice or game, drawing plays in my notebooks, visualizing myself on the court: seeing myself diving for loose balls and feeling the scabs on my knees burn; defending so closely my mark's knees and elbows leave bruises on my legs, arms, and chest; passing creatively, finding the open hands of my teammates; even making a few layups; Coach telling me I did well; Dad and Pop smiling proudly.

It's all sweaty practice and daydreaming until I'm suddenly playing our first real game against weak Rockport, and I'm actually *doing* all the things I visualized, which feels so amazing, I wonder if it's real – like maybe I'm sitting in science class just daydreaming.

But I'm not daydreaming in science class; I'm playing basketball.

I rack up fifteen assists while Terrell scores thirty-two points.

We're up by forty at the end of the third quarter, and so Coach puts in the second squad.

On the bench I notice my heartbeat slowing, my muscles cooling, and I begin to feel a wonderful sense of having completed a task.

I watch Boy21 play and again I can tell he isn't really playing. He doesn't make any mistakes, but he just looks to get the ball to the other backups so they can try to score. He's running at three-quarter speed; he doesn't shoot when he's open; there's no intensity.

He's playing very unselfishly, which is nice to see, but it also makes me feel as if he's hiding in broad daylight – like he's afraid to show the world what he can really do.

We win the game 101–69.

Dad is proud.

So is Pop.

TWENTY-FOUR

The second game of the year is the annual boy-girl doubleheader against Pennsville, our archrivals in basketball and by far our best competition for the conference championship. The day before the game, in practice, Coach has us all lined up sitting against the wall when he says, 'Based on our scouting reports, Pennsville's going to run what we'll call a triangle-and-two on Terrell, which means they're going to double-team him anytime he gets the ball.'

'Damn,' Terrell says. 'I hate being double-teamed.'

Coach ignores Terrell and says, 'Wes, Hakim, and Sir will experience a matchup zone, which will leave Finley wide open.'

What Coach means is that Pennsville doesn't think I can make my jump shots – they don't think I'm a threat to score. I'm not offended, because my being the weakest scoring threat on the team is a fact. I'm a point guard, not a shooter. That's my role, and other teams have doubled Terrell before, but for some reason my jump shot seems a little more off this year than in years past. I went zero for two in the first game.

'Finley will have to shoot his way out of the triangle-and-two,' Coach says. 'Which we all know he can and will do. He just has to hit a few early shots to make them switch to man-to-man coverage. And *then* we'll be able to run our regular man offenses.'

Coach teaches the second squad the Pennsville triangle-and-two defense, and then we practice against it. Just about every shot I take bounces off the rim. It feels like I haven't heard the sound of the ball spinning through net twine in years.

'Keep shooting,' Coach says. 'Get all your misses out today. Save your baskets for tomorrow.'

I keep shooting, but I feel a little more anxious with every miss. When I glance at my teammates, I see doubt in their faces – or am I just being paranoid?

Coach subs in Boy21 for me at one point and Russ misses all of his shots too, which doesn't make me feel any better. I'm really starting to think he's missing on purpose. This depresses me and makes me feel guilty, even though I told him not to hold back.

In the locker room after practice, Wes, Sir, and Hakim all punch my arm and pat my back and say things like 'You got all your misses out today' and 'Tomorrow's baskets are the ones that count, not today's' and 'Game day is the real day.'

But Terrell says, 'You better get that extra man off me early, White Rabbit. You hear? I want to hit a thousand points before the season's over.'

Coach is always saying we shouldn't chase personal records, but we all know there will be a huge celebration when Terrell scores his one-thousandth point. He needs me to do well if he's going to reach a grand this year.

I'm worried about tomorrow enough already, so my stomach flips and pulses when Coach calls me into his office. He shuts the door and says, 'I only expect you to shoot the ball when you're open tomorrow. You're a decent shooter, Finley. Hakim and Wes will rebound too. Trust me.'

'Yes, sir,' I say.

'Maybe talk to Russ about making more shots in practice too,' Coach says.

'So you think he's missing on purpose?'

'We haven't seen the real Russ play ball yet,' Coach says. 'And you don't know what a show you're missing.'

He looks into my eyes for a long time – like he's trying to control my mind or something – and I eventually look down at my sneakers.

'See you tomorrow, Finley.'

'Yes, sir,' I say, and then go change in the locker room.

I thought everyone had left, so I'm startled when I hear, 'Finley?'

Boy21 is standing next to me in a towel. He's the only player who uses those nasty showers, which haven't been cleaned for decades. He wears flip-flops to protect his feet.

'What's up?'

'I told my grandfather to pick me up at your house later tonight.'

'Why?'

'I was hoping we could sit on your roof.'

I sigh. I'm tired, and the thought of talking in code with Boy21 – all the cosmos and outer-space jazz – exhausts me. 'I have to do my homework.'

'We could do it together maybe.'

Russ is rubbing his chin over and over again, looking at me with these crazy intense eyes. Again, I wonder if he really has been missing his shots intentionally, and for some reason I decide he probably has. Something about the way he's standing – it's almost submissive, like a dog with its tail between its legs. Why would anyone yield to me?

TWENTY-FIVE

Dad heats up frozen pizza for us and Pop peppers us with questions about the Pennsville game plan.

'They're gonna double Terrell, right?' Dad says.

'Yep,' I say.

'Finley should get a lot of shots,' Boy21 says.

'Score some points for the Irish!' Pop says.

'For Bellmont,' Dad says. 'You think you'll get into the game, Russ?'

'Don't know.'

'You okay, Finley?' Pop says. 'You haven't touched your slice.'

Dad gives me a look.

I just shrug.

Boy21 and I do all our homework up in my room, but we don't really work together. He does his at my desk and I do mine on my bed for about an hour before we put our jackets on and go out onto the roof.

It's not really that cold out for winter. In the distance a police siren is whining, but it's a pretty peaceful night otherwise, and I always enjoy being on the roof, getting a different perspective. I start to zone out a little – in a good way.

After ten minutes or so of silence, Russ says, 'If I get into the game tomorrow, would you mind if I used my extraterrestrial powers?'

I'm not really in the mood for outer-space talk. 'The only way you're getting in the game is if I can't hit any shots.'

'You'll hit your shots.'

'Well, then it's a nonissue, right?'

'Guess so.'

I look up and see part of the moon sticking out from behind a cloud.

'I just want to know what I should do *if* I get in the game,' Russ says. 'Coach says he's going to give me some quality minutes whether I want them or not. You want to win the championship, so I figure it's best for me to use my extraterrestrial powers to help you beat Pennsville if I get the chance. I used telepathy to check with my dad up in outer space and he says it's okay if I expose myself a little bit, because he's coming soon to get me anyway.'

I'm tired of Boy21's outer-space fantasies. I'm tired of Coach pressuring me. I'm worried about my inability to hit a jump shot. And so I don't say anything in response. Silence has always been my default mode – my best defense against the rest of the world.

When Boy21's grandfather pulls up, I'm grateful.

'See you tomorrow,' Russ says as he climbs back into my bedroom.

I nod, but I don't leave the roof.

I hear Boy21 say good-bye to Pop and Dad, and then I watch him get into Mr Allen's Cadillac below.

As the taillights get smaller and smaller, I try to visualize myself hitting shot after shot, but I keep missing open jumpers, even in my mind.

TWENTY-SIX

The girls' game is before ours and the stands are packed. Because the girls are usually away when we are home and vice versa, this is one of the few times I'll get to watch Erin play this year.

I sit with my teammates in the designated spot in the bleachers and when Erin comes out I see that she's changed her jersey number to 18 – my new number.

I get a little emotional as the girls warm up. I start to feel exactly what I try to avoid feeling during basketball season – in love – and I'm equal parts happy and annoyed.

Wes and Boy21 are reading the next Harry Potter book. Wes fiddles with the zipper of his hoodie. Boy21 wrinkles his brow and nods every so often like he agrees with whatever he's reading. The rest of my teammates are listening to iPods or joking around. Coach Watts chaperones us.

There's a small section of Irish who've come to root

for Erin. They're sitting with Pop and our parents and they're all wearing green. One man has painted his face green, white, and orange like Ireland's flag.

But most of the people in the gym tonight are black because Pennsville is pretty much an all-black high school.

Erin opens the game by hitting a deep three pointer, which makes the crowd erupt. She looks gorgeous out there on the court and every time she does something good my teammates punch my arm or rub my head.

Erin hits shot after shot, pulls rebounds, get steals, and carries her team to a twenty-point lead by halftime. Just before she walks into the locker room, she looks up into the stands, finds me, and smiles.

She's so happy being out there on the basketball court doing what she was born to do – and I start to envy her, because I feel as though I might throw up.

I'm thinking about the triangle-and-two.

In the second half Erin blocks three shots, intercepts two passes, drives the lane several times for layups, comes off endless screens, sinks shot after shot, and secures the win easily. I'm happy for her, and I even smile back when she looks for me at the end of the game, but I still feel as though I might puke. Big-game jitters. This one could be for the conference.

As we stretch in the locker room, Boy21 seems calm. I think about how he'd be the perfect secret weapon tonight, and I want to tell him that it's okay to play to the best of his ability if he gets in the game – not to worry about me – but for some reason, I don't. Maybe I think he's not ready, or maybe I think he is and I just don't want to lose my starting position.

'Shoot your way out of the triangle-and-two early,' Terrell says to me. 'We both know the team's better when I'm the number one option on offense. Right, White Rabbit?'

'Right.'

I completely agree.

When they announce our squad, Terrell gets the biggest cheer by far, although I get a hearty roar from the Irish section. I see Pop parked in the handicap zone. He's wearing a green, white, and orange scarf. Dad's sitting next to him and a sweaty Erin is next to Dad even though she should be sitting with her teammates. I know that this is her way of being my girlfriend when I don't allow her to be my girlfriend, which makes me feel good, but I remind myself not to think about Erin tonight.

We're not dating during basketball season, remember?
Basketball is your girlfriend now.

The gym's rocking.

The students are chanting, '*Bell-mont! Bell-mont!*'

In the pregame huddle, Coach says, 'I don't think I have to remind you that this is a play-off game. We only play this team twice, and we need to win both times if we want to take the division and set ourselves up nicely for the postseason. Good man defense. Call out switches. Quick transitions, and shoot the ball, Finley. We need you to shoot your way out of the triangle-and-two.'

I swallow hard.

'On three, team. One, two, three—'

'TEAM!'

And then I'm on the court.

Wes wins the jump easily, and – just like Coach had predicted – Pennsville leaves me unmarked, double-teams Terrell, and sets up a triangle zone.

I know I'm supposed to shoot the ball, but I try to force it into Wes, which results in a turnover.

'Shoot the ball, Finley!' Coach yells.

The next time down on offense, when they leave me wide open, Coach yells, 'Shoot!'

I take a three pointer; it hits the front of the rim, and Pennsville gets the rebound.

I miss the next three shots.

We're down eight to nothing.

This isn't working.

I can't hit a shot to save my life.

'Keep shooting,' Coach says. 'Keep shooting, Finley!'

I try to get the ball to Hakim next, but I make another bad pass and suddenly I have two turnovers and four missed shots in a row.

I glance over at Pop and Dad and their eyes look small, their faces sheepish, like they're embarrassed for me.

'Keep shooting!' Erin yells. 'Keep shooting!'

The next time down Pennsville leaves me wide open, and I call time-out.

As I jog off the court, Coach says, 'Who told you to call time-out, Finley? *Who?*'

I swallow.

Coach looks me in the eyes.

He sees I'm rattled.

He sees I'm scared.

He says, 'Russ, report in for Finley.'

Russ doesn't make a move. Coach Watts grabs his elbow and sort of gives him a push in the right direction. Boy21 looks at me, but I look away.

As Russ reports in at the scorer's table, I become invisible – everyone is avoiding eye contact because they're embarrassed for me.

Boy21 takes my place on the bench with the starters.

'Same exact game plan,' Coach says. 'Russ – you're the shooter now.'

'Coach,' Terrell says, 'he can't shoot. We're already down eight.'

'You might be surprised,' Coach says. 'Now execute the game plan.'

'Finley,' Boy21 says. Everyone looks at me. *Everyone.*

'Do you want me to use my extraterrestrial powers to win this game?'

'What did he just say?' Terrell asks.

'Extra-*what*?' Sir says.

'Huh?' Hakim says.

'Russ!' Coach says. 'Not now!'

'Finley,' Boy21 says a little more slowly. 'Do you want me to use my extraterrestrial powers to win this ball game? Your call.'

'What the hell are you talking about?' Terrell says. 'We got a game to play!'

Boy21's staring at me – communicating with his eyes – and I can tell that he doesn't really want to do what he is about to do.

Part of me wants to see if he's the real deal.

Part of me just wants to beat Pennsville.

Part of me knows that I should've been encouraging my friend to use his talents all along and that I've been selfish.

The buzzer sounds.

The time-out is over.

'Finley,' Boy21 says, 'I need you to say it's okay.'

Finally I say, 'It's okay.'

Somehow I know this means I won't play again tonight.

'Okay, same game plan,' Coach says once more as I sit down on the other end of the bench and the rest of the team takes the court.

I feel ashamed being on the bench. Like I'm naked or something.

Everyone in the gym is watching the game, I know, but it feels like all eyes are on me. I begin to feel hot, anxious. I've never visualized being benched. This is not how things are supposed to be.

Sir inbounds the ball to Boy21 at half-court.

'Coach!' Boy21 shouts as he dribbles all alone, well behind NBA three-point range. 'You won't be mad at me if I use my extraterrestrial powers?'

My teammates on the bench are all whispering.

People in the stands are repeating Boy21's words to one another.

Somehow I know – everything is about to change.

Coach yells, 'Russell, just play ball like you can. *Please!*'

The Pennsville coach shoots a strange expression over to our bench.

And then it happens.

With no one on him, Boy21 pulls up for what amounts to a half-court jump shot.

As the ball arcs through the air, time slows down in my mind, like in a movie – I can see everything at once: the collective shock of my teammates, the expressions on the fans' faces, the mocking smiles of the opposing team.

Russ pulled up for a half-court shot with no one on him!

People are outraged.

How could a no-name kid coming in off the bench take a half-court jumper?

The audacity!

Who does he think he is?

But then the ball goes in – *swish* – and the crowd goes wild.

Boy21's face changes.

His eyes narrow.

His lips tighten.

His body loosens up.

He slaps the floor with his palms, gets into a low defensive stance, and waits for his man to reach him. When Pennsville's point guard crosses half-court, Boy21 guards him tightly and then steals the ball with ease.

He dribbles four times and then takes off at the foul line, spreads his legs, and soars.

Hanging there in the air, he looks like the famous Michael Jordan silhouette.

The entire gym rises up in anticipation and Boy21 dunks the ball with resounding authority.

If we didn't have breakaway rims, the backboard would have shattered into a million pieces.

My teammates on the bench are out of their seats, hooting, pumping fists in the air, hugging one another, going nuts.

JV Coach Watts has to pull a few of them off the court so we won't get a technical foul, and Coach gives me a glance that says, *Now do you understand what I was talking about?*

Pennsville calls time-out and their coach yells over, 'What the hell is this, Tim? Don't think I'm not going to check his records. This is shady. *Shady!*'

'Damn, Russ!' Hakim says.

'You really do have magic powers,' Wes says. 'I feel like I'm at Hogwarts.'

'We're gon' win this game,' Sir says.

Terrell gives me a look that says, *You knew, didn't you?*

'All right,' Coach says. 'Let's concentrate on the game plan.'

No one says a word to me in the huddle and I sort of fade into the background.

When the game resumes, Boy21 dominates.

He hits three pointers.

He pulls rebounds.

Runs fast breaks.

Dunks the ball.

Blocks shots.

Accrues steals.

It's like an NBA player decided to show up and play for our high-school team – that's how good Boy21 is. He's Andre Iguodala, playing against children. A man among boys. Players fall down like they have broken ankles when they try to guard Russ, because he's too quick.

Boy21 outruns, outshoots, outjumps, and outdribbles everyone on the court.

Soon we're winning easily – but the second quarter ends with me still on the bench.

While Coach and Mr Watts argue with the Pennsville coaches, who are demanding that the refs check Boy21's eligibility – as if Coach is expected to pull out a file containing Boy21's birth certificate and papers that document his entire life – the team goes into the locker room and peppers Boy21 with questions.

Why were you pretending that you couldn't play?

How'd you learn to play like that?

What was that you said earlier about having extra-terrestrial powers?

Where'd you come from?

What the hell is going on?

Boy21 sits on the locker-room bench listening to all of the questions with a very peaceful expression on his face.

If I didn't know better, I might say he looks smug.

But I know better.

He has two choices: he can tell everyone about his parents being murdered and his spending so much time in a group home for teens diagnosed with post-traumatic stress, or he can tell them about outer space.

I know what he'll choose before he even opens his mouth.

'I am called Boy21,' Russ finally says to the team. 'I'm a prototype sent to your planet to collect data on what you Earthlings call emotions. I'm not human, as you can clearly see when I play basketball to the best of my ability.'

All jaws drop.

Silence.

Wes squints like he's expecting me to put it all into context for him, but what would I say even if I were more of a talker?

'What the *hell* are you talkin' 'bout, Russ? Stop playin', yo!' Hakim says, and then everyone laughs nervously.

'You're not for real?' Sir says, smiling now, as if what Boy21 said was all a joke. 'You're just messin' with us, right, Russ?'

Boy21 shakes his head the way a father would at a little boy who doesn't understand something elementary, something simple that all adults understand – like why lakes freeze in the winter, or where babies come from.

'He's not playin',' Terrell says, looking very serious. 'He believes it. You can see it in his eyes. This fool's *crazy.*'

Boy21 just continues to smile sort of sadly.

Before anyone can say more, Coach strides into the room and launches into an explanation of his game plan for the second half now that Pennsville's out of the triangle-and-two and will be focusing more on Russ.

It's hard for me to listen to Coach talk about basketball.

I think about the newspaper photographers and reporters I saw standing at the end of the court – all the many classmates and neighborhood people who'll now be focusing their attention on the new basketball god in town. It won't be long before the word spreads and college scouts start coming – maybe even NBA scouts.

This might all sound overly dramatic on my part, but everyone in the room is thinking the same thing on some level after seeing what Boy21 can do.

We're going to win the state championship, and that's what matters most – not the fact that Boy21 is claiming to be from outer space.

While Coach talks, the smile on Boy21's face grows more and more strange, but he doesn't really seem to be paying attention to Coach, or to any of us – he's off in his own little world.

When we burst from the locker room and begin our halftime warm-up, I spot Erin staring at me with a very concerned expression on her face. I don't look up at Pop and Dad. I figure Coach will work me back into the game at some point, but I'm starting to feel pretty humiliated and pathetic sitting here on the bench, especially after all the work I did this past season and what I did to help Boy21 after Coach asked me to do just that.

But Coach doesn't work me back into the game.

Pennsville focuses on containing Boy21 in the second

half, which allows Sir, Hakim, Wes, and Terrell to score a lot of points.

We maintain a ten-point lead throughout, but Coach doesn't risk subbing in any of the bench – not even when Pennsville calls time-out with only a minute to go.

By the end of the game the finality of my position hits me and my eyes begin to burn. I feel as though I might start crying. As lame as it sounds.

My relegation hurts.

I love basketball more than anything.

I worked harder than anyone on the team.

I spent all that time with Boy21, just like Coach asked me to do.

And yet I rode the bench through one of the most important games of the year.

When we win and it's time to shake hands, the few reporters in the building rush Boy21 and ask him questions about who he is and where he came from.

'Call me Boy21,' he tells them, and then he points to the ceiling. 'I'm from outer space.'

Coach is arguing with the Pennsville coach, who shouts, 'The kid couldn't have just dropped from the sky! Why didn't anyone know about this Washington if he's a legit part of your squad? What did you have to hide? I'm protesting this game! This is bullshit!'

The students and parents have rushed onto the floor

and my teammates are celebrating like we've already won the state championship.

Boy21 is talking about the cosmos with a handful of very confused reporters.

My teammates are high-fiving everyone, yelling taunts, rapping, and even dancing. Parents and students are on the court. It's like a deliriously happy mob has formed, almost like it's New Year's Day or something. I should be celebrating too, but I can't.

I feel like I might freak out.

I'm not supposed to leave, but I slip out the back door and start running laps on the crappy track.

It's cold out, especially since I'm only wearing my basketball uniform, and suddenly I'm sprinting, although I'm not sure why.

I'm never going to get any significant minutes at point guard now that Boy21 has emerged as the best damn player in the universe – and I worked so hard. I can't imagine facing Pop and Dad later, having to tell them that I tried my best, but I'm no longer a starter. And I also know that things with Boy21 and me are going to change as well. No more being left alone, and how can I be his friend when all's I want to do is beat him out for the point-guard position? It's not fair.

And so I run harder, trying to stop thinking, turn off my mind, get the endorphins flowing, the heart pounding, and work off what I couldn't while sitting on the bench.

'Finley – wait up!' Erin sprints to catch up with me. 'You need to go back inside or Coach will suspend you for leaving before the team talk.'

'I can't talk to you,' I say. 'It's basketball season. We broke up.'

'Go back inside before Coach realizes you left.'

'Didn't you see how good he is?'

'I did.'

'Then why should I go back inside?'

'Because you worked hard. *We* worked hard. *You owe it to me.* Coach benched you because you stopped shooting, not because Boy21 is better than you. If you would've kept shooting in the first quarter when he told you to shoot, he would've worked you back into the game. But you didn't execute the game plan, Finley. He was disciplining you. And now you're acting like a baby, running out here all alone in the dark, freezing-cold night.'

Erin says all this while sprinting next to me, and for some reason her words make me pick up the pace until she stops running.

I sprint a lap without her.

She's right.

I *was* being disciplined, and I deserved it.

I *am* acting like a baby.

The sprinting relaxes me.

I want to tell Erin that she was amazing out there on

the court tonight, but I'm still upset, so when I reach her I just nod once and pant out warm silver clouds into the cold night.

Erin is shivering and I fight the urge to put an arm around her.

'Get your butt inside!' Erin smiles at me sort of funny. 'Hurry!'

I want to touch her. A roof night with Erin would feel fantastic right about now. My toes and fingers start to tingle. I'm glad when she lets me off the hook by raising her hand. I give her a high five and then run back inside, where the team is finally filing into the locker room.

Again, Boy21 sits with what could be mistaken for a very smug look on his face, but no one is asking any questions this time.

When Coach arrives he starts talking about what worked in the game and what we need to improve, just like he always does. He doesn't say a word about Boy21.

Coach talks some more about what we will be focusing on tomorrow in practice, and then he tells us that he's proud of the way we played as a team tonight, which is a little ironic because I only played a minute or so and the other twelve nonstarters in the room who *don't* think they are from outer space didn't get into the game.

When the talk is over we put our hands in the middle and yell *'Team!'*

As we disperse, Coach Watts stands between Boy21 and the rest of the squad, almost like he doesn't want anyone to speak to Russ.

Coach Wilkins asks me to meet him in his office, and when he shuts the door behind him he says, 'Russ is the new point guard, so if you want to get into the game, you had better shoot the ball when you're open. *Understand?*'

'Yes, sir.'

'You didn't execute the game plan, Finley. I had to bench you. Would've done the same thing to any other player.'

I believe that.

'You have anything to say?' Coach asks.

I think about it, and then say, 'I think he's pretending.'

'Come again?'

'Russ. He's just talking about outer space to keep people at arm's length.'

'I know.'

'He doesn't want to play basketball.'

'If he didn't want to play, I don't think he would have put on such a show tonight,' Coach says.

'I have a bad feeling about this, Coach.'

'We do the best we can, Finley. We can't change what happened to the boy's parents, but we can give him an opportunity to do what he's best at. He needs to play basketball – just like you do. Trust me.'

Coach has to believe he's doing the right thing because he doesn't know what else to do. I once heard someone say that everything looks like a nail to the man with a hammer in his hand. I thought it was just a corny cliché when I first heard that expression, but I think it actually applies to Coach right about now, which makes me sort of sad.

I want to play basketball and win the state championship.

I want to be the starting point guard.

I also feel like I should be helping Boy21, and I'm not sure Coach is right about Russ needing to play b-ball.

But I'm not the coach, and so I say, 'I'll shoot the ball when I'm told to shoot the ball from now on.'

'Good,' he says. 'See you tomorrow at practice.'

TWENTY-SEVEN

Dad left just as soon as the game ended. He had to get to work on time.

Because I want to be alone, I tell Pop that I'm going out for hot wings with the team.

Erin's parents take the old man home and I walk through the gray, dirty, trash-everywhere streets of Bellmont.

Almost all the streetlights have been smashed with rocks, so it's dark.

It's frigid out and I'm still in my shorts, with a winter coat on top. As I walk, I'm surprised that I'm not thinking about the game or losing my starting position.

I'm thinking about Boy21, and how bad he must be hurting.

People just don't go around saying they're from outer space for nothing.

The deep bass of an expensive car-stereo system approaches from behind. I turn my head, but all I see are two bright headlights. Somehow I know the car's going to stop, and it does just as it reaches me. The music turns off and I hear, 'Yo, White Rabbit, get in.'

It's Terrell's voice.

I walk to the passenger-side window. He's riding with his brother Mike. Both of them are wearing gold chains and huge diamond earrings.

'Don't just stand there lookin' at us,' Mike yells from the driver's seat. 'Get your lily ass in the car before you freeze it off in those ball trunks. Your knees look like snowballs!'

I open the back door and hop in, but Mike doesn't drive.

'You knew about this outer-space shit from the beginning, didn't you?' Terrell asks.

I don't see the point of lying, so I nod.

Terrell has turned his body so that he's facing me, but Mike's looking at me through dark sunglasses in the rearview mirror. It's after ten and he's wearing sunglasses. I smell some sort of sweet smoke in the air and then see that Mike is puffing on a joint. I want to get out of the car, but I know I can't.

'How crazy is he?' Terrell says.

'I don't know.'

'Crazy like he might come to school with a gun and start shooting people, or crazy like he just says amusing things about outer space?' Terrell says.

'The latter, I think,' I say.

'What you mean *the ladder*?' Mike says. 'You gon' climb a damn tree or somethin'?'

'So he's just all talk?' Terrell says.

'I don't really know.'

'Coach ask you to help him, right?' Mike says.

'Yep.'

'So you go and be his friend even though he gon' end up takin' your position?' Mike says.

'Right.'

'That's White Rabbit for you,' Terrell says.

'*You good people*,' Mike says, and then he takes a drag off his joint. 'I like you, White Rabbit. You got what the old people call *character*.'

'Russ is crazy as a mofo, but he makes us a better team,' Terrell says.

'I'm'a drive you home,' Mike says. 'You all right.'

I don't want to let Mike drive me home because he's high, but there's nothing I can do about it, so I just sit quietly in the backseat. When one of the most feared drug dealers in the neighborhood wants to drive you home, you let him drive you home. I know he's strapped. There are probably several guns in the car, and who knows what's in the trunk.

We pull up to my house, and just before I get out, Mike says, 'You need any paper, White Rabbit?'

'Money,' Terrell says when I don't answer.

I shake my head no.

'Let us know if your family ever needs paper,' Mike says. 'You can always work for us. We like to employ people with character.'

I nod once, even though I never want to be a drug runner, and then get out as fast as I can.

When Mike and Terrell drive away I go inside and find my grandfather drinking a beer.

My dad's already at work, so it'll be just Pop and me tonight.

'You feel like shit, don't you?' Pop says.

'Yeah.'

'Well, you shouldn't. Your father's always telling you that you can outwork talent, but I got a news flash for you, Finley. You could work as hard as you humanly can for the rest of your life and you'll never be as good as what we saw tonight.' He takes a swill from his bottle and says, 'I fancy a bath. You game?'

I nod and push Pop into the bathroom, where I strip the old man and lift him into the tub.

As I hold the detachable showerhead for Pop, he washes his hair, and I watch the suds run down his neck and over Grandmom's green rosary beads. Pop won't even take them off to bathe. When he finishes, he tells me to turn off the water and when I do he says, 'Coach will work you into the games. Don't worry. It'll work out.'

I'm wondering what Boy21 is thinking right now. Did

he enjoy playing tonight? Did it make him feel better? Does basketball help him the way it helps me? And, if so, does he need the starting position more than I do?

'I love watching you play ball, Finley. Best part of my days lately – makes me feel like I still have legs, even – but life's more than games. This Russ, he's special. Anyone can see that. And it's hard to be special, Finley. *You understand what I'm saying?*'

I don't understand what Pop is saying, but I nod anyway.

'You're special too, Finley. You don't always get to pick the role you're going to play in life, but it's good to play whatever role you got the best way you can,' Pop says. 'And I know I'm a damn hypocrite for saying that tonight, but that don't make what I said a lie. We've both had hard lives so far. No favors done for either of us.'

I can't think of anything to say, especially since I'm not special at all, so I just get Pop out of the tub and into bed.

I lie awake all night thinking about what has happened and what it all means.

TWENTY-EIGHT

The next day, just as soon as his grandfather drives out of sight, Boy21 reaches into his over-the-shoulder bag and pulls out a brown robe made from bath towels safety-pinned together. He slips his head and arms through the holes.

On his chest he has spelled the word SPACE with red fabric that looks like it was once a T-shirt.

He then ties a sparkly gold cape around his neck. The cape looks store-bought and expensive, as it has a silver clasp and the material is much heavier than what might be used to make a cheap Halloween costume.

I just stare at Boy21 when he puts on a motorcycle helmet that he has spray-painted silver. He's glued a golden eagle to the top of the helmet – the kind of eagle you might see at the end of a flag post in a classroom.

I wonder why he hid the robe and cape when his grandfather must have seen the helmet, but I don't ask, of course.

'No more Russ Washington,' he says. 'It's Boy21 everywhere I go now. The time to leave Earth is soon. No point in lying about everything now. They've all seen my extraterrestrial powers anyway.'

I give him a look that says, *You sure about this?*

Boy21 ignores my look and says, 'And after practice I'd like you to listen to a special CD that will explain everything. I'm going to ask Wes to join us as well. Will you listen to the recruiting CD with me?'

I nod.

What type of CD could explain everything?

I want to know. But I also realize that Boy21 is losing it – *or is he?*

Students mob us as we approach the high school. They want to know why Boy21's wearing what he's wearing, where exactly in outer space he came from, and how many points he'll score in the next game.

The best-looking girls blink a lot, say, '*Hey*, Boy21,' blow him kisses, and even reach up to touch his silver helmet in a sexy way.

It's almost unbelievable, especially if you don't know how popular basketball is in Bellmont.

More and more people crowd around us, but Boy21 just keeps moving forward with this very eerie smile on his face.

Who knew that acting like a total freak would make you popular?

Or is it just because he's an extraordinary basketball player?

As everyone continues to press in around us and yell questions, I start to feel invisible because no one says a word to me, even though they obviously know Boy21 and I are tight. No one ever said much to me before, but now that Boy21 has appeared, it makes me realize that maybe he has something I don't. Not only athletic ability, but also star power, no pun intended.

When we finally arrive at the high-school steps, he stops and says, 'I will score many, many points in the next game – definitely more than forty, guaranteed. And I come from a place that you don't even know exists. I will be returning to that outer-space place shortly, and anything else you might learn about me will come through my Bellmont Earthling tour guide, Finley, who will also serve as my Earthly documentarian.'

Most of the students surrounding us laugh as if Boy21 is joking, but I can see Erin twenty people deep in the crowd, and she's biting down on her lip.

'Finley,' Boy21 says, 'please tell the masses all they need to know about Boy21.'

Everyone turns and looks at me, but, of course, I don't speak – because I'm a minimal speaker, yes, but what would I say, even if I were a blabbermouth?

'No fair!'

'White Rabbit never says *anything*!'

'How do you run basketball like that?'

'We wanna know what you playin' at!'

'What's up with that spaceman *outfit*? You in the Black Eyed Peas now?'

'Who *are* you?'

'I'm Boy21 from the cosmos!' Russ says, and then he turns so quickly that his sparkly gold cape flies up into the air.

I march after him into the building.

The questions continue all day.

Boy21 just smiles and smiles and repeats the same standard lines about coming from the cosmos to learn about emotions.

The less he says to our classmates, the more popular he seems to become. Everyone wants to know his secret, and that's his power – just having one.

The local papers don't run any information about Boy21 except the number of points he scored in the game, and his assists and rebounds. The editors were probably too scared to report what Russ actually told them, but I wonder how long it'll be before his real story comes out and he'll have to face the truth about his past.

Our teachers don't ask Russ about his costume, which leads me to believe that they were instructed not to, because he looks absolutely ridiculous – like an insane person dressed up for Halloween or the Mummers Parade or something even crazier.

I worry about lunch, when we'll see the rest of the

team without the close supervision of teachers, but we're called down to guidance and separated just before it's time to eat.

Boy21's instructed to head into Mrs Joyce's office, and I'm directed to Mr Gore's.

Mr Gore's Jheri curl is extra shiny today.

'I had a lunch sent up,' he says when I sit down in front of his desk. 'Go ahead and eat.'

I look at the hot turkey sandwich.

White bread.

Tan-yellow gravy.

It looks good.

I'm hungry, so I eat.

'Have you figured out yet why Coach picked you to help Russ?' Mr Gore says.

I shake my head no.

Mr Gore smiles broadly – too broadly, as if every single one of his teeth is calling me a liar.

He touches his fingertips together and keeps tapping the tops of his palms so it looks like a spider is doing push-ups on a mirror.

'Tell me something, Finley.' Mr Gore looks deeply into my eyes, until I look down at my food. 'How did your grandfather lose his legs?'

I hate it when Mr Gore asks me irrelevant questions – especially this one in particular.

I feel my face burn like it always does whenever I'm

in his office. I hate this feeling I get when I'm forced to listen to his pointless, stupid questions.

'Don't you think it kind of odd – your not knowing the answer to that one? Have you never thought to ask him how he lost his legs? All these years, it's never crossed your mind to ask?'

My hands are balled into tight fists. He's trying to make me upset so I'll talk, and I don't like it.

'What happened to your mother?' Mr Gore asks.

I'm starting to get really annoyed with this line of questioning, especially since guidance has a student who says he's from outer space in the next room.

What is the point of these questions?

I'm sweating now.

Don't lose it, I tell myself. *Do something productive to take your mind off of what's happening.*

I work on consuming my hot turkey sandwich. I take huge bites and enjoy the feeling of swallowing. My stomach begins to feel full. I savor the taste of meat and gravy and doughy bread.

'Finley?' Mr Gore says. 'Are you listening to me?'

I nod without making eye contact.

'So what do you think we should do about Russ?' he asks.

'I don't know.'

How should I know?

'How're *you* doing?' he asks.

'Fine.'

'Are you upset about losing your starting position?'

I shrug.

'It's okay to be upset.'

I quickly eat the mashed potatoes and drink the milk.

I want out of here.

'Do you want to know how Mr and Mrs Allen were murdered?' Mr Gore asks, which surprises me.

'No.'

I don't want to know that.

Why the hell would I want to know that?

'Can I leave?' I ask.

'It's okay to feel upset, Finley. This is a lot for you to process. It's more than most young people could deal with. I just want you to know that I'm here to listen, should you ever feel like talking about Russell – or yourself. I'm a resource for you. A safe ear.'

'Thanks,' I say, but I'm already walking toward the door.

When I exit, Mr Gore all but yells, 'It might help Russell if you told him about your mother.'

I don't want to think about what he's implying, so I just leave Mr Gore's office and take a seat in the hallway outside the guidance department offices.

I clench my fists and then stretch out my fingers as wide as they will go.

I repeat that process over and over again until I calm down a little.

Boy21 comes out a few minutes later, but he doesn't say anything to me.

He looks unfazed.

He's still wearing his brown robe, gold cape, and silver helmet.

I follow him down the hallway to our lockers. The hall monitor hassles us, but Boy21 remembered to get a pass, so we're okay.

We trade in our morning books for our afternoon books and then Boy21 says, 'They don't want me to wear my outer-space clothes. They say it disrupts the school day. Do you agree?'

'No,' I say, which surprises me and makes Boy21 smile.

I didn't like my conversation with Mr Gore, and that makes me apt to disagree with anything guidance has to say.

'Maybe I can get my parents to beam down another outer-space cape for you, Finley,' Boy21 says. 'Would you like that?'

'Very much so,' I say and then smile.

We finish our day, and then we attend practice.

Boy21 takes off his space clothes and puts on a practice uniform so that he looks simply terrestrial instead of extraterrestrial.

When no one on the team brings up outer space or

anything Russ said last night, I figure Coach must've talked to all the other team members and instructed them to stay mum.

Boy21 invites Wes to listen to the CD with us after practice, saying it's a little like N.E.R.D., because it's related to outer space, and Wes agrees, although he quickly changes the subject by saying, 'I need to work on my free throws.'

So we shoot some free throws until Coach shows up and runs us through a regular practice.

I run with the second team, and that relegation stings a little, although I try to rise to the challenge of playing against our best players and I'm able to lose myself in sweat, aching muscles, and the repetition of the drills.

'Looking good today, Finley,' Coach says more than once, which makes me feel a little better.

After we grab our gear in the locker room, Boy21, Wes, and I hop into Mr Allen's Cadillac.

'You want me to drop you boys off at home?' Mr Allen says.

'They're coming over to listen to an important CD,' Boy21 says.

'They are?' Mr Allen looks at us in the rearview mirror. Brown eyes. Gray eyebrows. 'What CD?'

'It's something for school,' Boy21 lies. 'Mostly about science.'

'Okay, then,' Mr Allen says.

When we arrive at the Allens' home, Mrs Allen insists that we each shower up, put on our school clothes, and sit down to dinner. 'I didn't know you were coming, but we'll make do,' she says, which is nice, so we all grab quick showers and then eat a chicken salad dinner.

Wes is very polite and carries the conversation as the Allens ask us about basketball and school.

'We're reading *Le Petit Prince* in French class,' Wes says. 'You might like that one, Russ, come to think of it, because it's about a boy from another planet.'

Russ says, 'I'd like to read that.'

Mrs Allen gives Wes a hard look – I guess she doesn't want us to encourage the space fixation – and Mr Allen says, 'Basketball is going well?'

'Fine,' Wes says. 'We have a good team this year. Coach thinks we can go deep into the postseason.'

'That so?' Mr Allen says. 'Any new defenses? A press perhaps?'

Wes tells Mr Allen all about our playbook – both what we have used already in games and what we haven't. They talk hoops for a long time while the rest of us listen.

With Wes around, I feel like I can be myself and remain quiet. The Allens never ask me a direct question, and Wes is very talkative by nature, so it's an easy dinner.

A few times I catch Mr and Mrs Allen staring at Russ's space robe and cape. There's a sadness in their eyes. Boy21 doesn't wear the helmet to dinner.

'We will go to my room now,' Boy21 says when we finish dinner, 'and listen to that CD for school.'

'Okay,' Mrs Allen says. 'Study hard.'

'Excellent meal, ma'am,' Wes says.

I nod in agreement.

And then we follow Boy21 up into his room, where the walls and ceiling are now entirely covered with glow-in-the-dark stars, which seem to pulse energy. It's a little bit eerie and disorienting but also kind of beautiful, in an odd way.

'Sit on the bed,' Boy21 says when he closes his bedroom door.

We sit and then Russ begins to pace.

'So,' Wes says, 'let's hear this CD.'

'Can you guys keep a secret?' Boy21 asks.

'Sure,' Wes says.

'You know it,' I say.

'I used to do this thing with my dad,' Boy21 says – he's still pacing. 'And I've never told anyone about it before.'

'What thing?' Wes says, and then he glances at me nervously, which makes me wonder if Wes somehow found out that Russ's parents were murdered.

'Back home in California, he used to drive me out to where there are no houses or lights, so that we could see lots of stars. We used to drive to this place on the coast. A little cliff that overlooked the Pacific Ocean. We'd park and walk along the edge until we couldn't see the road anymore – so that car lights wouldn't break the mood.'

Boy21's pacing slows a little.

'We'd throw down a blanket to lie on and put the CD player between our heads, and while we stargazed Dad would play this music.'

He holds up the CD.

The cover features a black man wearing a crazy pharaoh-looking outer-space outfit and a long cape. Behind him are stars and what looks like Saturn, maybe – a planet with a ring around it.

'It's called *Space Is the Place* and it's the sound track to a movie that my father says is pretty bad, although I've never seen it. It's by the jazz musician Sun Ra and his Intergalactic Solar Arkestra. Sun Ra claimed that his music could transport people to outer space. I was hoping that maybe we could pretend we were looking up at the stars and listen to the CD together. See what happens. Just like Dad and I used to do.'

Wes looks at me sort of funny, and I shrug to let him know that I'm game.

Why not?

Especially since it might help explain why Russ needs to be Boy21.

Plus I'm really curious to find out what such music might sound like.

'Okay,' Wes says, but he sounds hesitant.

Boy21 smiles and stops pacing. 'You're going to love this. *Space Is the Place!* Okay, lie down on the floor. Get comfortable. Look up at the stars. And don't talk until the entire CD has finished playing. That's the one rule. You'll know when the experience is over because I'll turn on the light.'

Wes gives me another doubtful glance, but I'm already lying on the floor, so he follows my example.

Boy21 pulls the blinds and turns off the lights so that his stars glow a weird green, and then he presses Play on his CD player and lies down between us.

The CD opens with strange outer-space noises and a woman chanting, *'It's after the end of the world. Don't you know that yet?'*

Then there are very strange pulsing noises and squealing echoes that sound like a trumpet being tortured to death.

But as I look up at the green constellations, I get the feeling that I'm really in outer space, which is weird, because how would I even know what that feels like?

The rest of the CD features long African drumming sessions.

What sounds like a piano crashing down flights of stairs.

Sun Ra preaching about the 'alter destiny' and 'the living myth' and powering his spaceship with music – all over strange noises that sound more like a computer malfunctioning than jazz.

A woman sings nicely for a time, about 'a great tomorrow', and is encouraging us to 'sign up with Outer Space Ways Incorporated' if we 'find Earth boring.'

Then there is a song about Pharaoh being on the throne when the black man ruled the land, and I wonder what that has to do with outer space, but I sort of realize that the whole record is about black culture and how it might thrive more easily in the cosmos.

The music sounds nothing like N.E.R.D. at all, but it's very interesting, and as I lie there listening, gazing up at Boy21's fantasy outer space, I feel as though I'm in a trance or something, and I actually do imagine myself traveling through distant galaxies, which is pretty cool.

I've never taken drugs, but I wonder if taking acid might feel something like listening to *Space Is the Place* in the dark while staring up at glow-in-the-dark sticker constellations.

The last song is the title track and it's upbeat and makes me feel like I really want to go to outer space, where 'there's no limit to the things that you can do'.

After listening to this CD, it's easy to see where Boy21 is coming up with his weird philosophies and costumes.

Wes and I don't make a sound through the entire experience, and when it's over, Boy21 turns on the lights.

Wes and I sit up and blink.

'Now that was different,' Wes says while making a lemon face, as if he's really saying, *What the hell was that?*

Boy21 says, 'So what do you think?'

'About what?' Wes says.

'Outer space. Do you want to come with me?'

Wes raises his eyebrows. 'Where exactly do you think you're going?'

'Saturn and then beyond,' Boy21 says. 'Black man and the cosmos! That's where my parents are now.'

'Finley too? Or is space only for black people?' Wes says.

I note the sarcasm in Wes's voice.

'Finley has a calming presence,' Boy21 says. 'We'll make an exception. He'll be our token white space traveler.'

I smile. All of this is insane. Russ could be kidding, pretending, messing with us. But Wes is uncomfortable.

'Okay,' Wes says. 'We'll go to outer space with you. When are we leaving?'

'Sooner than you think,' Boy21 says.

'Right,' Wes says. 'Got it. Now Finley and I have to go. Homework and all. We'll see you tomorrow morning?'

'Very well,' Boy21 says. 'I'm so glad that you'll be making the journey with me. We can listen to Sun Ra some more to get used to being in outer space. We'll practice being in the cosmos again soon.'

I want to talk to Russ about the music and why he and his father used to listen to it on the cliff, under the stars, but Wes has already exited the room and he's my ride home, so I'll just ask Russ tomorrow, when we're alone. It's easier to talk when it's just Russ and me anyway.

Downstairs we say good-bye to Mr and Mrs Allen.

'Do you want a ride home?' Mr Allen asks.

'I live just around the corner,' Wes says. 'My pop'll drive Finley home.'

A block away from the Allens' home, Wes says, 'I think this is serious. That music was nuts. I can't believe I lay there for all that time listening. He's either psycho or messing with us.'

I'm surprised Wes didn't think it was an interesting experience.

'Or he's just doing what he has to do to get through the day,' I say.

'What do you mean?'

I don't get to answer because I hear someone screaming my name. I turn around and see that Boy21 is sprinting toward us, his cape trailing.

'Finley! Finley! Wait up!'

Wes and I look at each other; he's just as concerned as I am. When Boy21 reaches us he puts his arm on my shoulder and pants for a few seconds.

'What's going on?' Wes says.

'My grandfather's coming to pick us up.'

I see the headlights of Mr Allen's Cadillac coming toward us now.

'I told you,' Wes says, 'we don't need a ride.'

'Coach just called,' says Russ, still panting. 'There's been an accident.'

'What happened?' Wes says. 'Just say it.'

Russ ignores Wes, puts his other hand on my shoulder, and looks into my eyes. I see the Russ I saw on his birthday, when he was talking about his father on my roof – the real Russ. Not Boy21.

'It's Erin,' Russ says. 'She's in the hospital. She was hit by a car.'

'What?' Wes says. 'How?'

'Don't know,' Russ says.

Someone's jabbing a finger in my throat again; I can't breathe.

Mr Allen pulls up, rolls down the window, and says, 'Come on. Get in.'

I'm sliding through the worst streets of Bellmont now, seeing my blank reflection in the window – my face superimposed on our shitty neighborhood.

Breathe.

Try to breathe, I tell myself.

But it's getting harder and harder.

'What happened?' I finally get the words out. 'Is she okay?'

But no one answers, not even Mr Allen, which seems bad.

Really bad.

ERIN

'If you have the words, there's always a chance that you'll find the way.'

Seamus Heaney

TWENTY-NINE

Mr Allen drops Russ, Wes, and me off at the emergency room and then goes to park his car. The automatic sliding doors close behind us and I throw up in the waiting-room trash can.

It feels like I'm turning inside out.

When I come up for air, half the room is looking at me. There's maybe twenty or so sick, weary people sitting in chairs, and one homeless man pacing at the far end of the room, yelling, 'Whenever I get help, I'm gonna be thankful! Whenever I get help, I'm gonna be thankful!' The other half is watching a show about sharks on the TV that hangs in the corner. I glance up just in time to see the massive jaws of a great white clamp down on a sea lion.

Russ puts his hand on my back and says, 'You all right?'

I puke again and just look up at my teammates when I finish.

I don't know how I am.

'Listen,' Wes says, 'you're going to have to lie and say you're family, or they won't let you in. I know, because when my sister had her baby her friends tried to come in during the birth, and the hospital people said only immediate family could visit. So tell them you're Rod. They're probably not going to let Russ and me in, so you have to get yourself together.'

Wes's hand is on my back now too. He says, 'You need to be strong for Erin. Be a man. *Okay?*'

I nod because I'm supposed to, but I feel like I'm going to throw up again.

At the main information desk, Wes tells the woman that I'm Erin's brother and, just like he predicted, he and Russ are made to stay in the waiting room, while I'm led to what the check-in person calls the trauma center.

I stand in the doorway for a few seconds before I enter Erin's room.

It's like a nightmare.

Her left leg is in a soft cast and there's a plastic neck brace holding her chin in a very rigid position.

Her right arm's all wrapped up.

There are red bandages on her face that were once white.

The skin around her eyes is purple and black.

Her face is really puffy and shiny; it looks like someone smeared Vaseline under her eyes.

Mrs Quinn's sitting next to the bed, which has wheels on it, so maybe it's not a bed. I don't know.

They're holding hands.

Erin's moaning and her cheeks are wet with tears.

'I'll leave you alone with your family,' the nurse says.

I stand frozen for a long time, just watching, wondering if this can be real.

Erin looks ruined.

Mrs Quinn's hair is all frizzy and wild and her eyes look small and scared. She's staring at the window even though the blinds have been pulled. Neither Erin nor her mother notices me at first.

I walk around to the far side of the bed and take Erin's other hand in mine. She doesn't squeeze.

When we make eye contact, it doesn't even look like her, because of the swelling, but I recognize the shamrock-green eyes.

She starts talking really quickly. 'Finley, my leg's shattered. I'm never gonna play basketball again – *ever*. It's over. That's it. My season's ruined. My basketball career is over. No chance for a college scholarship now. When they hit me, they knew it. They saw my face. I flew up onto the hood of their car. I was thrown onto the street – and they just left me there like I was a dead animal. It seemed like they even sped up when— But that can't be true, right? Who would do something like that? And now I can't play basketball. *What am I going to do about college?* How are we going to get out of Bellmont *now*? I should have made my decision and committed earlier. How could they leave me there? I don't want you to see me like this, Finley. I must look so ugly. Maybe you should leave. No, don't leave. And the paramedics cut through my brand-new sports bra too – I just got it two days ago – and that bra cost a lot of money, and—'

'Shhh,' Mrs Quinn says. 'You're in shock, honey. You'll be playing basketball in no time. We'll get you a new sports bra. It's going to be okay.'

So many thoughts are running through my head, but I can't seem to make sense of any of them.

'It hurts, Finley. It hurts so much. I can't move my leg.'

When Erin starts to sob, she looks like a little kid who's been tortured to the point of exhaustion. I can see the pain tunneling its way through her face and body.

It hurts for her to even cry.

I want to tell her it'll be okay – that she'll be playing ball again soon.

I want to ask her how she got hit – what happened?

Will she ever be able to walk again, let alone play basketball?

I look to Erin's mom for help.

'She can't have painkillers until they rule out any possible head injuries. They're going to scan her brain

194

soon, and then – once they rule out brain damage – they'll give her drugs,' Mrs Quinn says. 'You just have to hold on a little longer, Erin.'

'What about her leg?' I ask. 'What did the doctor say about that?'

When Mrs Quinn doesn't answer my question, I study her face. She looks very scared herself. Suddenly, I understand that it's probably worse than I initially thought.

'Finley,' Erin says.

Her eyes are red, but the green shines even now – even amid all the swelling and bruising – maybe even more so.

'Will you please be my boyfriend again?' she says. 'I need you to be my boyfriend now. I'm scared. I'm really scared. Please be my boyfriend again. I can't go through this alone. Please. *Please.*'

I nod.

Of course I will.

'I need you to say it,' she says, and her voice sounds tiny and childlike and so unlike Erin that I really start to worry.

'I'm your boyfriend again now,' I say.

'Then talk to me. Tell me something else,' she says.

'Like what?'

'Anything to take my mind off the pain.'

'I just threw up before I came in here.'

'Really? Are you okay?'

'Wes and Russ are in the lobby. Boy21 made us lie on his bedroom floor in the dark and listen to this jazz CD about using music to travel through outer space and then I was confused and suddenly I'm at the hospital and I was so worried about you that I just threw up. I puked twice. I puked yellow bile even.'

'Very romantic. You really know how to make a girl feel special, Finley,' she says, which makes me feel good because she smiles for a second. 'I've missed you. Look what I have to do to get your attention.'

She tries to laugh, but the attempt hurts her and she starts crying again.

I'm afraid that Erin might die, because she looks that bad. 'It's going to be okay.'

'No, it's *not*. It's really *not* going to be okay, Finley.' Erin tries to laugh, but only starts to cry harder.

Her mom strokes her forehead and says, 'Shhh. It *is* okay. Everything's fine.'

Because I don't know what else to do, I start to pet Erin's hand like it's a cat or something. After a minute or so, she yells, 'Just everyone stop touching me – *okay?*'

Mrs Quinn flinches.

I try to make eye contact with Erin, but she's staring fiercely at the ceiling; I can tell that she doesn't want to look at me all of a sudden and that I should just be quiet.

We wait around silently for a long time, until they take Erin into a room where they will scan her brain.

Mrs Quinn's allowed to accompany her, but a nurse tells me to stay behind.

Being alone in a hospital freaks me out so I return to the ER waiting room to see if Wes and Russ are still there.

I find them with Mr Allen, watching a show about snakes. On the hanging TV a snake with a head as big as a football is in the process of swallowing what looks like a dog, although I can only see the hind legs sticking out of the snake's mouth. I wonder why they play these types of shows in the ER waiting room, where people are already feeling depressed about hurt loved ones. Couldn't they find more lighthearted programming?

Mr Allen, Wes, and Russ stand when they see me. Russ is no longer wearing his cape.

'How's Erin?' Mr Allen says.

I shake my head and say, 'Not good.'

'What's wrong with her?' Russ says.

'Her leg's shattered and she has bruises all over her face. They're scanning her brain for damage now. She was rambling for a time and then she got really angry and started yelling at me like I did something wrong, when all I was doing was holding her hand.'

'The girl's in shock,' Mr Allen says. 'Won't last. She'll be back to normal soon.'

'Sorry to hear that,' Wes says. 'Damn.'

Boy21 says nothing.

I look up and the snake has finished swallowing. Its midsection is now the shape and size of the dog; it almost looks fake.

'I'm gonna stay here,' I say. 'You guys can leave. Thanks for waiting.'

'You sure?' Wes says.

'Yeah. I can catch a ride home with the Quinns if I need to.'

'Tell Erin we're pulling for her,' Russ says.

'Yeah,' Wes says, 'please do.'

'We'll pray for her tonight,' Mr Allen says.

'Thanks.' I go back to the trauma center, but Erin and her mom are still in the brain-scanner room.

Alone in the hospital, I think about how fragile people are, how anyone can disappear in a second and be gone forever – how close I've come to losing Erin – and I start to remember things I don't want to remember, so I bite down on the triangle of skin between my left thumb and forefinger until it hurts enough to stop my brain from dredging up any of the garbage that sits at the bottom of my memory.

When Erin's wheeled back into the room, she has an IV drip in her arm and is semiconscious.

'Her brain's okay,' Mrs Quinn says. 'She's on morphine now.'

I pull up a chair and hold Erin's hand.

'I'm your boyfriend again,' I tell her.

'That's good,' she says, and then smiles once before she closes her eyes.

THIRTY

Eventually Coach shows up with the girls' coach, Mrs Battle, a large squat serious lady who always wears a tracksuit. Tonight she has on a navy-blue number with three silver stripes running the length of her arms and legs. Erin's mother and father repeat all the information we know.

Hit-and-run.

Shattered leg.

Major reconstructive surgery.

After the Quinns explain the metal external fixator – a superskeleton on the outside of Erin's leg that will hold the bones in place – there's silence.

What else is there to say, really?

Erin's season is over.

Coach shakes his head sadly.

Mrs Battle frowns and says, 'Tell Erin the team will visit,' as if that will really help.

Everyone nods sort of dumbly and then Coach says, 'Finley, I'll drive you home. Let's give the Quinns some time to themselves. Erin's drugged and out for the night. There's nothing for you to do here.'

I look at the Quinns and see that the wrinkles around their eyes are pink and raw. It does look like they want to be alone, so I nod and follow Coach out of the hospital.

We say good-bye to Mrs Battle in the parking lot and then get into Coach's truck.

The Bellmont streets silently pass by the passenger window. I see a man sleeping on the sidewalk. A small abandoned bonfire in an oil drum makes an alley glow. Hookers in wigs, short skirts, and fur coats are pacing under the overpass.

'I have to take care of my pop,' I say, just to break the silence. 'I have to put him to bed.'

'I'm taking you home,' Coach says, but that's it; he doesn't say anything else, which makes me feel sort of strange.

It's late, so Dad's already left for work.

Coach tells Pop about the hit-and-run – how Erin was walking home from practice and a car came around the corner just as Erin was crossing the street, hit her, and then sped away.

Pop just shakes his head, grabs onto the crucifix at the end of Grandmom's rosary beads, and says, 'I hate this neighborhood.'

I get the old man's diaper changed, carry him upstairs, and then put him to bed. When I turn out the lights, Pop says, 'What did Erin tell you about the accident – anything that Coach left out?'

'Just what we told you.'

'Nothing else? *You sure?*'

I think about it, replaying Erin's words in my mind. 'She said they might have sped up before they hit her.'

'That's what I thought.' The old man shakes his head and blows air through his broken, jagged teeth.

'What?'

'Maybe this wasn't an accident.'

'What are you saying, Pop?'

'You're not stupid, Finley. Stop pretending you don't understand what's going on.'

I think about what the old man means and immediately dismiss his words as crazy. *Why would anyone want to break Erin's leg?*

Back in the living room, Coach has helped himself to one of Pop's beers and is sitting on the couch.

'Wanted to speak with you,' he says.

Before I can think better of it, I say, 'Do you think that maybe someone hit Erin intentionally to get back at Rod?'

Coach opens his eyes really wide. He looks at me for a moment, and then he says, 'Don't know, and I don't *wanna* know, either. *You* don't wanna know that, Finley.

Haven't you lived in this neighborhood for eighteen years? Don't go there. Useless information. Not a damn thing to do with thoughts like that. You hear me?' He takes a sip of Pop's beer and says, 'Sit.'

I sit.

'I'm real sorry about what happened to Erin. It's a shame. A damn shame.' Coach looks down at his hands for a few moments, but when he looks up, he's smiling, which makes me feel very weird. 'In other news, the cat's out of the bag. You don't have to keep Russ's secret anymore.'

In other news? Did Coach really just make that transition?

'I'm already getting calls from top programs. Coach K phoned just this morning. Coach K himself. Duke basketball. Russ really has a shot to go far, and your helping him get through this tough period is commendable. I want you to know that I appreciate it very much and that you'll be getting your minutes, don't you worry. I know this is a tough night for you, Finley, and that's why I wanted to say I'm proud of you. You did a good thing, helping Russ. But the job's not done yet.'

I just stare at Coach. I know that he's trying to make me feel better about losing my starting position, that he's thanking me, but with Erin in the hospital – with my having just seen how bad she was hurt and understanding that her hopes for a college scholarship are now over – this hardly seems like the appropriate time to be discussing Russ.

My hands are balled and I can feel my face getting hot.

'I just wanted to take that off your mind, in light of all you have to think about now, with Erin in the hospital,' Coach says. 'I'm not displeased with you. Quite the opposite. And the doctors will fix Erin's leg. Don't worry about the rest. You can't control the rest. So just forget about those questions you were asking earlier. Okay?'

I nod, because I don't want to continue this conversation.

Coach sips his beer once more before he places it on the coffee table and says good-bye. Then I'm alone.

I stretch out on the couch and wait for my father to come home so that he can advise me, but I fall asleep somewhere around three.

I sit up when I hear the front door open.

I blink.

'Finley?' Dad says. 'Why are you sleeping on the couch?'

My face must look terrible, because Dad sits next to me and says, 'What's wrong?'

After a minute or so of waking up and thinking and remembering, I tell him what happened.

Remembering is bad, but it feels even worse to say the words.

My stomach starts to churn.

I feel guilty, but I'm not sure why.

It's confusing.

Finally I say, 'Do you think that someone hurt Erin because of who Rod is and what he does? Do you think that it might not have been an accident?'

Dad looks scared. His left eye is sort of twitching. 'Someday you and Erin are going to leave this neighborhood and never come back. May that day come soon.'

He didn't answer my question directly, but I know he's talking in code, the way people do around here. So he's confirmed my suspicion.

'Go get your pop ready for his day, and I'll put on breakfast.'

And so I do.

THIRTY-ONE

Boy21 emerges from his grandfather's Cadillac looking very much like an Earthling. He's wearing dark jeans, a Polo rugby shirt with the huge oversize polo-player-on-a-horse symbol, and a cool leather jacket – no robe, cape, or helmet. Judging by the look on his face I don't think I'm going to hear anything about outer space today.

'Hey, Finley,' he says. 'You okay?'

I nod.

'You hear anything more about Erin?'

I shake my head.

'My grandparents are praying for her.'

'Thanks,' I say, even though I'm not sure I believe in praying, mostly because Dad, Pop, and I stopped going to church when I was a kid.

'I'm sorry that Erin's hurt so bad and won't be playing basketball.'

'Me too.'

'Do you want me to sit tonight's game out?'

I look at Russ and say, 'Why would I want you to do that?'

'I don't know.'

'I heard Coach K called about you.'

'I've met Coach K a half-dozen times,' Russ says, as if Coach K were just any old person and not the head of perhaps the best collegiate basketball program in the country. 'At camps.'

This means that Russ has been to summer invitation camps for the best high-school players in the nation. They get to go for free and meet all sorts of basketball celebrities.

'Why are you here?' I ask. 'I mean, you could be anywhere. Any prep school in the country would take you. What are you doing here?'

'I wanted to be near my grandparents,' Russ says. 'Besides . . . maybe I *need* to be in Bellmont.'

'This hellhole? Why?'

'To be your friend,' he says.

I don't understand why he would say that, so I just let it go.

I'm tired, and we've reached the high school. As we go through the metal detectors, people start asking me questions about Erin. I return to silent mode.

All day long I think about Erin and how strangers

are operating on her leg, cutting it open, inserting pins or whatever to mend the bones. I worry that the surgeons won't get it right and Erin will have to walk with a limp, or even worse. I can't pay attention in any of my classes. And when I receive a slip that says to report to guidance during my lunch period, I don't even mind the fact that I'll have to speak to Mr Gore, because it means I won't be around Russ. He keeps asking me if I'm okay and it's getting really annoying.

When I sit down across from Mr Gore I notice the Duke bumper sticker above his filing cabinet and start to get mad, although I'm not really sure why.

'You okay?' Mr Gore says.

I shake my head.

'You want to talk about anything?' His Jheri curl is looking a little flat on the left side – like maybe he slept on it and didn't have time to do his hair this morning.

'I'm tired of Bellmont,' I say.

'What do you mean?'

'I'm tired of seeing graffiti every day. I'm tired of drug dealers. I'm tired of people pretending that they don't see what's going on in the neighborhood. I'm tired of good people getting hurt. I'm tired of basketball. I'm tired of doing nice things for people and being punished for it. I just want to get out of here. I just want to escape.'

The words simply popped out, which surprises me. Mr Gore seems surprised too, especially since I never talk to him about anything important. He's trying not to smile, but I can tell he thinks he's making progress with me. Maybe he is.

'Are you tired of Erin?' His eyes are all excited now.

'No.'

'And yet you broke up with her for basketball.'

'What does that have to do with her being in the hospital?'

'Absolutely nothing.'

'Why did you call me down here?'

'Because I care about you.'

Mr Gore's leaning forward. His forehead is damp, like he's nervous – or maybe like he really does care. When I look into his eyes, I see something that makes me feel as though maybe I was wrong about him all along. It's hard to explain. It's been a strange twenty-four hours, and I didn't sleep much last night.

'You know, I played high-school basketball,' he says.

'Really?' I find it hard to believe, because Mr Gore is very thin and fragile-looking, but he *is* tall.

'Played in college too, until I hurt my knee. I used to be able to dunk.'

I try to picture Mr Gore dunking and the little movie I create in my mind makes me laugh.

'As a young man I dedicated my entire life to basketball, and you know what basketball does for me now?' he says.

'What?'

'Nothing.'

I think about what I'll be doing when I'm Mr Gore's age and I can't see myself playing ball. Even if I went pro, I'd be done playing. For some stupid reason, I see myself with Erin – maybe we're married. We're all old and silly-looking – somewhere far from Bellmont, somewhere decent – but we're still together. I wonder if we really will be.

'You don't owe anything to Coach,' Mr Gore says.

I just look at him for a second. He seems different to me, like he's on my side. Maybe I've had him all wrong. And his saying that about Coach makes me feel better, for some reason.

'You look tired, Finley.'

'I didn't sleep much last night.'

'You want to catch a few z's in my office?'

'Are you serious?'

'I'm in meetings this afternoon. If you want to take a nap, you can do so here. I'll let your teachers know that you're with me. Just don't go telling anyone my office is a hotel.' Mr Gore shoots me a corny wink, and then adds, 'We good?'

I don't know if I'll be able to sleep in his office, but I would like some time alone, so I say, 'Thanks.'

'No problem. I'll be in the conference room next door if you need me.'

He pats my shoulder twice before he exits, and then I'm alone.

I stare out the window for two hours and think about Erin.

Halfway through the last period, I slip out of the building before Russ or anyone else can find me.

THIRTY-TWO

I walk around the crappy Bellmont streets for a few hours before I return to the high school to watch our JV team play.

When I pass him in the stands, Terrell says, 'How's your lil baby doin'?'

I stop and look into Terrell's eyes. 'Don't call her my lil baby. You know she doesn't like that. She's told you hundreds of times. Show some respect,' I say, hearing the anger in my voice. It surprises me.

'Okay, Finley,' Terrell says. *'Damn.'*

Hakim and Sir exchange a glance, and then continue to watch the JV team play.

Terrell was just trying to be nice, and I feel a little guilty for yelling at him, but I'm also glad that he called me Finley and not White Rabbit, which seems important. So I add, 'Don't ever call Erin my lil baby again. Okay?'

'Relax, Finley,' Terrell says. 'Watch yourself.'

I know Terrell means I'm stepping out of line, that I've ignored the power structure here in Bellmont, that I should know my place or else I'll be reminded, but I don't really care about all that right now. First my starting position was taken from me, and now Erin. What else matters?

I sit down.

Russ slides toward me and says, 'Where'd you disappear to during lunch?'

'I was with Mr Gore,' I say, and then stare at the JV game. Our team is already losing by fifteen. Coach Watts calls time-out and is now screaming at his starters about running an offense. 'Any offense!' he yells.

'You all right?' Wes says.

'Yeah,' I say. 'I just wanna watch the game, okay?'

Wes and Russ glance at each other, and then they leave me alone. So does the rest of the varsity team.

When the JV squad finishes, we shoot around – I hit every shot I take – and then in the locker room Coach announces the starting lineup, leaving out my name. No one says anything to me about my demotion, and I really don't care all that much.

During warm-up drills I see Pop and Dad in the stands, and I think about how Dad has his car with him. I could walk right over to him and say, 'Let's go to the hospital to check up on Erin.' He'd say I should play the game, that I made a commitment to the team. But he'd take me if I pressed him.

Russ gets the biggest roar by far when they announce the starters. Terrell looks at his sneakers. Coach's talk about *the team* will sound a little different to Terrell now that he's no longer the number one option.

I'm standing behind Coach as he goes over the game plan – how to beat Brixton, tonight's opponent – but I'm not really listening at all.

Then I'm on the bench watching Wes win the jump ball, which he tips to Russ, who dribbles toward the basket. He dishes the ball to Hakim, who scores an easy layup.

'Red twenty-two,' Coach yells, and the team drops into a 2–2–1 press.

I think about Mr Gore saying basketball means nothing to him now. I suddenly realize I don't care whether we win this game, or if I even play. It's a game. Erin's in the hospital. *What am I doing here?*

I never dreamed I'd stop caring about basketball, but I really couldn't care less about it right now.

I stand and say, 'I'm sorry, Coach. I have to go.'

'What?' Coach says. 'Where?'

I stride past the opposing team, right up to Pop and Dad.

'I should be at the hospital,' I say. 'I want to be there when Erin wakes up.'

Coach Watts has followed me. 'Finley, you best get your butt back on our bench.'

Pop looks at Coach Watts and says, 'He's got a lady in need.'

'You know that there will be consequences,' Dad says.

'Last chance, Finley,' Coach Watts says.

All the people in the stands are staring at me like I'm a complete freak.

The opposing coach calls a time-out to set up a press break, and, as my teammates jog off the court, they stare at me too. I see concern on Russ's face.

'I should be at the hospital, Dad.'

'Okay,' Dad says.

I push Pop's wheelchair out of the gym and the night is more than refrigerator cold – it's freezer-cold now.

We get into the car and Dad drives.

'I'm proud of you,' Pop says. 'People are more important than games.'

'I'm sorry,' Dad says, because we all know my leaving means Coach has every right to never play me again. If I had simply asked to miss the game before it started, Coach would have probably let me go spend time with Erin, no problem. But leaving the bench in the first quarter is unheard of. Dad and Coach both know that it means I basically just quit the team.

'It's okay,' I say, and then exit the car.

'Take this,' Dad says, handing me a twenty-dollar bill. 'Call me when you're ready to come home, but if it's after I go to work, take a cab.'

We don't have a lot of money, so twenty bucks is a big deal. It's Dad's way of saying he's okay with my decision – that he supports me.

I tell the hospital people I'm Erin's brother and I'm allowed in, even though it's not regular visiting hours.

'Your parents are in the cafeteria,' a woman says and then points me in the right direction.

I find Mr and Mrs Quinn staring at coffee cups.

They look up at me with tired eyes.

'Don't you have a game tonight?' Mr Quinn says.

'Can I see Erin?'

They nod.

'Just try not to wake her if she's still sleeping,' Mrs Quinn says. 'She needs her rest.'

Mrs Quinn gives me the room number and when I find Erin her eyes are closed.

Very quietly I stand next to her bed and watch her breathe.

The swelling in her face has gone down considerably.

The IV drip in her arm means she's heavily drugged.

Her bad leg is locked in a slightly bent position and – through the sheet fabric – I can see things poking through, which I imagine to be part of the metal skeleton that will hold her leg together as it mends. I don't want to see the damage just yet, so I don't peek.

I think about running with Erin, sprinting, climbing out onto my roof – her using her knee in all sorts of ways.

Almost anything can be ruined. Everything is fragile. Temporary.

Because I can't help it, I lean down and kiss her forehead once, and I think I see her smile for a second in her sleep, but it's dark so I can't be sure.

'You shouldn't be in here,' a nurse whispers from the doorway. 'She needs her sleep.'

I nod.

I kiss Erin's forehead once more. There's a notepad and pen on the table next to the bed, so I scribble a quick message:

I was here.
Love,
Finley

I follow the nurse, who says, 'She's your classmate?'

'My girlfriend.'

She nods once before she says, 'You're a lucky man.'

'I am.'

I want to go sit with the Quinns, but for some reason I go to the waiting room instead, and watch all the people who have kids staying overnight at the hospital or who are waiting for loved ones to wake up from surgeries or whatever. They all look just as concerned as I probably do. I see a mom and a dad holding hands, comforting each other. An elderly woman talks to a priest for a while.

And a little kid sleeps with a teddy bear in one arm and his thumb in his mouth. So many people with problems and hurting, sick family members.

Just before they make us all leave, I look in on Erin once more. She's sleeping comfortably, so I take a cab home.

THIRTY-THREE

The next morning over eggs and bacon, I ask Dad if I should skip school to check on Erin. Before he can answer, Pop says, 'Yes.'

'Have you missed a day of high school yet?' Dad asks.

'Nope. Perfect attendance. So what's one day?'

Dad looks at me and says, 'You sure you don't want to talk to Coach?'

'I think the team will be just fine without me.'

'Okay,' Dad says. 'I don't like you quitting anything, but under the circumstances . . . I just wanted to make sure you're okay with the consequences, that you won't regret the decision later. I mean, you love basketball, Finley.'

'Erin's more important. Right?'

Pop pulls two bucks from his shirt pocket, holds the money out to me, and says, 'Buy Erin some flowers, will ya? Tell her I'm looking forward to the next game of War.'

'Thanks, I will,' I say, even though flowers will cost more money. It's a nice gesture and I appreciate it. He's probably been holding on to those two bucks for years. My dad pays for everything around here, and Pop hasn't worked a day since he lost his legs.

On his way to school, Russ shows up at my front door, once again looking very terrestrial. It's like Boy21 really has left the planet.

'I'm going to the hospital today,' I say. 'Not going to school.'

'I'm really sorry about how everything's turned out, Finley. Truly.' He's cracking his knuckles one at a time.

'I have to help Erin now. Okay? Stick with Wes in school. He'll get you through.'

'It's about more than getting through,' Russ says. 'Can we talk later tonight?'

'I don't know.' I have no idea what will happen at the hospital. 'I have to go. See you later, man.'

Russ nods once and then heads for school. He looks lonely, walking all by himself, but there's nothing I can do about that now.

Dad drives me to the hospital and we buy flowers at the gift shop near the cafeteria. I pick out a single yellow rose in a plastic vase because I know Erin likes yellow and the arrangement is the cheapest they have. I use Pop's two bucks and Dad covers the rest.

We walk to the part of the hospital where Erin's recovering and tell the woman behind the desk that we're here to see my girlfriend. I don't have to lie about being Rod because there are visiting hours in this part of the hospital.

She looks at a chart briefly, runs down a list with the tip of her pen, and says, 'Erin Quinn's not seeing visitors today.'

'I'm her boyfriend,' I say.

'Sorry,' the woman says.

'Can you take this to her and let her know I'm here?' I ask. 'She'll want to see me. She'll tell you so. I swear.'

'The patient has requested that no one except her parents be permitted access to her. Those are her wishes.'

'She's not a patient,' I say, fully realizing how ridiculous it sounds, because Erin *is* a patient. 'She's my girlfriend.'

'Maybe so. But she doesn't want to see you today. Come back tomorrow. Maybe she'll have changed her mind by then.'

'Can we send her a note through you?' Dad asks.

'We can do that.' The woman sighs as if we're asking her to do a hundred push-ups, or something equally insane.

'Do you have any paper?' I ask.

The woman stares at me for a second over her neon-green reading glasses, and then she slaps a pad of paper on the counter.

I hesitate but then say, 'You wouldn't happen to have a pen, would you?'

She shakes her head with enough force to set her neck fat in motion, but she hands me a pen. I wonder why she's so angry, but then someone behind me says, 'This is asinine! Why can't I go in to see my daughter? I'm tired of waiting here!'

The woman behind the desk probably has to listen to people yell all day.

I write:

Erin,

Pop sends you this flower. He's looking forward to the next game of War. I skipped school and am in the waiting room. Tell them to let me in and we'll talk.

Love,
Finley

I fold the note in half and stick it between the stem and the white cotton-looking plant they stuck in with the rose.

When the woman finishes speaking with the yelling man, she gestures to me and says, 'Take a seat. When things slow down a little, I'll have one of the nurses deliver the flowers to your girlfriend. If she wants to see you, we'll let you know.'

'How long will—'

'Don't know,' she says without looking up from her lists and charts.

'Come on, Finley,' Dad says, and we sit down in the waiting room, where a half-dozen people are watching *Good Morning America*. Some singer I don't know is performing outside in the streets of New York City. When she sings, you can see her breath. She doesn't look much older than me, and here she is on TV. How does that happen?

Dad falls asleep while we wait, and I wonder if Erin really doesn't want to see me. I start to worry. I feel confused. I can't imagine why I was denied access to her.

Finally, Mrs Quinn appears, looking very tired and unshowered – probably because she spent the night at the hospital – and says, 'I'm sorry, Finley, but Erin doesn't want to see you today.'

'Why not?'

'She's tired from the surgery, and she's not looking very well either. You know how girls are about being seen without makeup.'

Mrs Quinn is lying, trying to soften the news. Erin never wears makeup. She doesn't even *own* makeup.

'It was nice of you to bring the rose. It really brightened the room.' She hands me a note, and then leaves.

It's Erin's handwriting.

You shouldn't have left your game last night. You should be in school right now. Forget about me. Apologize to Coach and enjoy the rest of your basketball season. Don't come back to the hospital. I can't see you.

Erin

I keep reading Erin's note over and over again, but it doesn't make any sense. Just the other night, she practically begged me to be her boyfriend again, and now she says she can't see me?

I start to feel sick to my stomach.

I don't know what to do, so I just sit there waiting, hoping Mrs Quinn will return with a smile on her face and say, 'Just kidding!' But Mrs Quinn doesn't return.

Good Morning America ends. Some talk show begins and Dad snores through it all, right next to me.

He wakes up around lunchtime and says, 'How's Erin?'

I show him the note.

'She's probably angry about what happened. She's not in shock anymore. She's feeling the full effect. But she'll come around.'

'Do you mind if we stay here?' I say. 'I'd like to stay, just in case she changes her mind.'

'I can sleep anywhere,' Dad says, and then shuts his eyes.

After school ends, Mrs Battle and the girls' team

come with balloons and cards, but they aren't allowed in either, which really makes me worry about Erin.

When I tell her Erin wouldn't see me, Mrs Battle says, 'Well, then, we might as well get back to the gym for a late practice.'

Erin's teammates look sort of pissed off, which makes me angry, because it's not like Erin invited them to a party, right?

They leave all the get-well gear at the desk and file back out to the bus.

Dad and I eat dinner at the cafeteria.

'You know,' Dad says, chewing a bite of hamburger, 'Erin's family might be trying to protect you, Finley.'

'What do you mean?'

'Whoever hit her, well, maybe they're watching,' Dad says, and then he glances around the cafeteria carefully.

'I don't care about any of that. I'm done with that stuff, Dad.'

'You can't just be done with it,' he says. 'It doesn't work like that.'

'Erin and I didn't ask to be a part of that world.'

'Neither did I,' Dad says, which makes me feel bad, because Dad's life has been pretty bleak, and through no fault of his own. 'All's I'm saying is to give it time, and don't do anything stupid. You and Erin can leave Bellmont someday. You can go far away. Like I should have done with your mother.'

This is the first time Dad has mentioned Mom in years. 'I thought we weren't supposed to talk about Mom.'

'We're not.' Dad finishes his hamburger, and the conversation ends, because I don't know what else to say.

There's a different nurse at the desk now, so I try one more time to see Erin. I'm denied access again, so I let Dad drive me home.

Pop's drinking a beer and watching the Sixers game. 'How's Erin?'

'She refused to see us,' Dad says.

'We sent a yellow rose in to her with a note,' I say. 'I told her the flower was from you, Pop, and that you wanted to play her in War.'

'It's a lot to take in, a loss like that. She'll come around,' Pop says. 'Here's some strange news for you. Russ is up in your bedroom, Finley.'

'What? Why?' I ask.

'Something about stars,' Pop says, and turns his attention back to the TV.

Dad and I exchange a confused glance before I jog up the steps and into my room.

When I open my bedroom door, Russ is standing on my desk chair, with his hand in the air like the Statue of Liberty.

It takes a second to register, but then I realize he's in the process of turning my bedroom ceiling into a galaxy.

He's already covered two-thirds of it with glow-in-the-dark stars.

'*Surprise?*' Russ says halfheartedly when he sees me.

'What are you doing?'

'I wanted to do something nice for you,' Russ says. 'So I bought you your own cosmos.'

In spite of all that has happened, I smile. No one has ever purchased and arranged a galaxy for me before.

'Wanna help me finish?' Russ says.

I nod, and then we're taking turns standing on my chair, arranging constellations. It feels good just to have something to concentrate on. And when we've covered the entire ceiling, Russ shuts off the lights. We stretch out on the floor and bask in the weird green glow.

'So how's Erin?' Russ says.

'Not good,' I say. 'She wouldn't see me.'

'Why?'

'Dunno.'

'Give her a few days. Sometimes people need time and space.'

For a few minutes, we just look at the weird constellations we made.

'Coach says you come to practice tomorrow, all will be forgiven,' Russ says. 'No questions asked. No punishment for missing today's practice or for leaving the game.'

'Is that why you came tonight? To deliver Coach's message?'

'No,' Russ says. 'I came to put up the stars. I came to make you feel better.'

'I don't know,' I say. 'I mean, thanks. I appreciate the kind words. But I feel like Erin needs me now. I wish there was something I could do for her.'

'When I was in the group home a woman used to read to us at night. I would just sit and listen. I couldn't even tell you the names of the books, but it helped. I never told that woman I liked it when she read to us, but I did. Maybe you could read *Harry Potter* to Erin? Maybe she'd like to escape to Hogwarts?'

'Maybe,' I say.

It feels nice to hang out with Russ – especially after all that's happened. It's almost like we can pretend we're still kids or something – and I wonder if that's also why we like reading kids' books like *Harry Potter*. I don't know.

I'm glad Russ came to my house.

I'm glad he made me a galaxy.

THIRTY-FOUR

Every day Dad drives me to the hospital and I walk up to the desk with the first Harry Potter book in my hand, ready to take my girlfriend to Hogwarts. And every day the nurse says Erin doesn't want to see me. So I sit in the waiting room, frustrated and angry.

Mr Gore says that if I keep going faithfully, eventually Erin will let me in. When I ask how he knows, he says, 'True love always wins,' which sounds corny, but I hope he's right.

I don't go to basketball practice, which means that I officially quit the team.

Coach doesn't come see me, nor does he send any messages through Russ, and I wonder if he's mad at me. Or maybe he's just happy to have Russ playing for him. Maybe in his eyes I already served my purpose. It's funny how one violent event can make you see the world so differently. When a mobster runs down your girlfriend with a car, basketball just doesn't seem so important anymore. And Coach's talks about figuring out life on the court sound like so much bullshit now. Or maybe I did figure out life through basketball – people care about you if you can help them win, and they don't care about you if you can't.

After a week or so, the nurse says Erin has been moved to a different building for rehab. 'What building? Where?' I ask. But they tell me it's confidential, which makes me mad enough to sprint back into the ward to see if they're lying to me.

'Erin?' I yell when I reach her old room, but there's an old lady sleeping in the bed where my girlfriend should be.

A huge security guard grabs me by the arm and says, 'I suggest you exit the premises quietly and without incident.' He escorts me to the door, saying, 'Don't come back.'

Because I have no cell phone, I walk across the street to the pay phone outside the Wawa, but of course someone has pulled the phone part off, so I have to wait outside the hospital in the freezing cold until Dad returns to pick me up.

I start hanging out across the street from the Quinns' house. I just stand on the sidewalk all afternoon, waiting for Mr or Mrs Quinn to come home, so that I can ask them where Erin is, but I don't see them for days. I even get up in the middle of the night and walk down the street just to see if their car is in the driveway. It isn't.

A week or so later, a FOR SALE sign pops up in front of their row home, and shortly after, large angry men start transporting the Quinns' furniture into a huge moving truck.

'Where are you taking all this stuff?' I ask the men.

'Can't say,' says a guy with a spiderweb tattoo on his cheek.

Another guy with a thick red scar across his neck says, 'You best move along. *Now.*'

Pop and Dad say that Erin is obviously being relocated, but by whom and why, no one knows.

I ask Mr Gore if he's heard anything. He checks the computer system at school, which states that Erin is being taught by home tutors. He doesn't know anything else.

I go to the gym one day and confront Coach before practice is supposed to begin. 'What do you know about Erin?' I say, because he knows almost everyone in the neighborhood and he hears things. 'Do you know where she is?'

'How would *I* know anything?' Coach shakes his head, and then says, 'I told you not to ask too many questions. Be careful, Finley. And I'm sorry things worked out the way they did, but you made your choice.'

He turns his back on me, which lets me know he doesn't want any part of the Irish mob and won't be getting involved. He's done with me. After all I've done for Russ, I have to fight the urge to shove Coach. I feel so betrayed, even though I realize there's not much Coach could do to help me, even if he were willing to take the risk.

One night at four in the morning, when the neighborhood is asleep, I break into the Quinns' row home. There's no moon; I can't really see. They used to leave a key under the third brick in the garden, so I fumble around on my hands and knees, counting bricks and sifting dirt until I find that key.

All the blinds are pulled, so once I'm inside I can use a flashlight without being seen.

But there's nothing left – not even a piece of trash.

Nothing.

I shine the light on every inch of floor in every single room; I check every closet; I even look in the attic and basement.

No trace of the Quinns remains.

It's like they vanished.

I start to feel like I might puke again.

I stand in Erin's room, and it still smells like her. Peach shampoo. Her vanishing seems impossible. She would have contacted me if she were allowed, which means she probably *couldn't* contact me. I sit down on the pea-green carpet in the middle of four indented circles where the bedposts used to be. I hold my head in my hands.

Where could Erin be?

How did I lose the best part of my life?

I feel alone in the world.

When I leave, I keep the key, although I'm not sure why. Maybe just to have some part of Erin with me.

I walk around in a daze for a few days, not answering anyone's questions about how I'm holding up.

I can't think about anything but Erin.

I get so nervous about her whereabouts that I lose my head and barge into the Irish Pride Pub one afternoon after school. I don't consider the consequences; I just stride in. It's a last resort, and the only place I can think of where I might find Rod Quinn.

A half-dozen men in black leather jackets are sitting at the bar drinking beer.

I walk around the pool tables toward the men, and the bartender sees me first. He's got gray hair and a crooked nose. But he has kind blue eyes that seem to be telling me to turn around and leave before the men on the stools see me.

'Excuse me,' I say.

Everyone turns around. No one smiles.

'May I please speak to Rod Quinn? It's important.'

The men squint at one another in a way that lets me know I shouldn't have mentioned that name.

The bartender says, 'Hey, kid. Time to go.'

'I'm looking for Rod's sister, Erin,' I say. 'She's my girlfriend.'

'You shouldn't have come in here,' one of the men says.

'Know your place, McManus. Don't be like your grandfather. Be like your dad.'

'I just want to know where Erin is.' I'm sweating now and my hands are shaking, but I don't care about what might happen to me. I need to find Erin.

One of the thinner and clean-shaven men grabs the back of my neck, marches me over to the pay phone on the wall, drops two quarters into the machine, and says, 'Call your father and tell him where you are.'

'Where's Erin?' I say.

'This isn't a game, kid.'

'Where is she?'

He squeezes the back of my neck so hard that my knees buckle. 'Call your father. I'm the nice one here. If those boys at the bar become interested in you, you'll be very sorry.'

I punch in the number for my home and Pop answers.

'Pop, I need Dad to pick me up.'

'Where are you?' Pop says.

When I hesitate, the man says, 'Tell the old legless man where you are.'

'I'm at the Irish Pride Pub.'

'What the hell have you done, Finley?' Pop says.

'Can Dad come pick me up?'

The man takes the phone from me and says, 'Come

pick the kid up, and don't let this happen again.' He hangs up and then pushes me outside, where he lights up a cigarette.

We stand on the sidewalk for a few minutes before I say, 'Where is she?'

'You really got a thing for Rod's sister, huh?'

'I love her. She's my best friend.'

'That's cute,' he says. He flicks his butt into the street and lights up another cigarette. 'If you want to see her again, I suggest you let things quiet down. Talk to your grandfather. He understands how these things work.'

'Can I just talk to Rod? *Please.*'

'You really don't quit, do you?' he says. 'You have no idea how lucky you are that I was sitting at that bar today.'

My dad pulls up, gets out of the car, and says, 'Lewis?'

'This one belong to you, Padric?'

Dad swallows once and nods.

'He busted into the joint and started making demands about his girlfriend, so I straightened him out before the others could. But had I not been around, this story doesn't end so happily.'

'Thank you,' Dad says, and then extends his hand. Lewis shakes and then pulls Dad in for a man hug. As he pats Dad's back once, Lewis whispers something into my father's ear.

'Get in the car, Finley,' Dad tells me. As we pull away, he says, 'What were you thinking?'

'What did he whisper in your ear?'

'That I now owe him a favor. Do you know what that means?'

I nod. It means that my father will have to do something for Lewis in the future.

'Lewis is an old friend. We grew up together. So you got damn lucky today. But you have to stop. You can't keep asking questions. You have to be patient.'

I don't *want* to understand any of what he's saying. I'm just a kid. I'm not part of the Irish mob, or whatever they're calling themselves these days – or whatever they're *forbidding* people to call them.

When we get home, Pop's wheelchair is parked at the kitchen table. Grandmom's rosary beads are wound around his fist, but he's not drinking and looks sober. The old man is shaking his head at me. 'Are you *crazy*?'

'I—'

'You can't know where Erin is right now!' Pop roars. 'Are you fecking stupid, boy? Have you not been lookin' at these stumps of mine for a decade now? What's wrong with you? Those men you approached today would slit your throat for a dollar.'

Pop's never cursed at me like this before. His voice is shaking. I've never seen him so angry. His accent's even coming out. *Feck.*

Dad puts his hand on Pop's shoulder and Pop lets out a terrible sigh.

'Listen, Finley,' Pop says, calmer now. 'Sometimes a guy can get out of the organization by doing something big. Something that earns him a retirement. If Rod did something big, he might've made some powerful enemies that would require him and his family to disappear. Could be that they didn't disappear fast enough, which maybe explains Erin's accident. This is all speculation, Finley. Don't go repeating any of this. You have to be smart. I know Erin. She'll contact you when it's safe. But your going around asking questions only makes things difficult for everyone.'

I look at my father and he nods. He thinks Pop's right.

'So I should just wait for Erin to contact me?' I say. 'Do nothing?'

'That's your best play,' Pop says.

'And your safest,' Dad says. '*Our* safest.'

How can I do nothing?

THIRTY-FIVE

One morning, on our walk to school, Russ asks me to shoot around in my backyard – just the two of us. He says it could be 'our thing.' I ask him why we need a 'thing' and he says, 'You seem different, distant – not yourself. Maybe shooting around once or twice a week would help?'

He stops by later that night after his practice and I tell him I don't really want to shoot around with him. 'I'm done with basketball,' I say.

'Just take ten shots and if you don't feel like taking an eleventh, I'll drop it forever, okay?'

I sigh.

'Come on,' Russ says. 'Just ten shots.'

I follow him around the house and we find my ball in the garage.

'I feel bad about taking your position,' Russ says. 'Especially after what happened to Erin. Her accident – the way she disappeared . . . it really affected me. Sort of woke me up. I don't know why, but that night in the hospital something clicked in my mind, and then it was like I started moving forward again and you started moving backward. Now it feels like we're moving in opposite directions, and I miss having you around all the time. Everything got messed up for you, and yet things are going so well for me now, or better than I thought was possible at the start of the school year. It doesn't seem fair.'

I don't know how to respond, so I don't. He's right, of course. I've been mulling over the unfairness of my situation for weeks, but hearing Russ state it so matter-of-factly hurts. Part of me is jealous. Part of me is simply defeated.

'The thing is – Coach was right,' Russ says. 'Playing basketball's been really good for me. I like the structure. I like playing. It takes my mind off what happened back in L.A. It's my future too. I want to thank you for seeing me through my transitional phase.'

Is that what he's calling his outer-space act now? He's all but forgotten about being Boy21. It's like basketball was his cure – his return to sanity.

'I think that playing ball could help you too,' Russ says. 'I realize you're done with Coach, I get that – but maybe *you and I* could—'

'It's just a game. Maybe it's *your* ticket to fortune and fame – and I'm happy for you – but I don't care about basketball anymore. *I really don't.*'

'Just take ten shots. I bet you'll want to take an eleventh,' Russ says, spinning the ball in his hands.

'Fine,' I say, and then show a target. He hits me in the hands and I shoot. The ball goes in. Russ rebounds, passes to me, and I shoot again. We repeat the process, find a rhythm, and I start to feel my heart beating, my muscles loosening. I miss shots five and seven, and end up eight for ten.

'So?' Russ says.

I think about it. I understand why Russ needs to play ball. I understand that the game is going to provide him with many opportunities. I even understand why it's helping him mentally – keeping his mind off the bigger questions. But basketball isn't going to do the same for me. And shooting around is just a painful reminder that Erin's no longer here.

'Won't be taking an eleventh shot,' I say.

'I'm sorry,' Russ says. 'I don't want basketball to be a sore spot between us.'

'It's not.'

'So what now?'

'I'm going to lie on the garage roof and stare up at the few stars I can see,' I say.

'Can I join you?'

'Sure.'

We use the fence to help us climb up onto the garage

and then we look up at the three or so stars we can see through the light pollution and smog.

'You ever feel like you're not the person on the outside that you are on the inside?' Russ asks.

'All the time.'

'Yeah, me too,' he says.

We lie there in silence.

'I'm sorry basketball's ruined for you,' Russ says.

'I'm glad it's helping you,' I say, and I really am.

THIRTY-SIX

The days pass very slowly and superfast at the same time.

Do you know what I mean?

Maybe it's like a dream where time takes on a new sort of meaning.

I don't know.

Life gets blurry, distorted, stretched out, balled up. It's hard to explain.

I go to school.

I do my schoolwork.

I talk to Pop, Dad, Russ, Mr Gore.

Things happen, but nothing really sticks in my memory.

Nothing worth mentioning anyway.

I just feel numb all the time.

Empty.

Sad.

Sometimes angry.

Mostly sad.

Kind of pissed.

Hollow.

Tired.

Cheated.

Lonely.

I think about Erin constantly.

Where could she be?

Is she somewhere better?

Will she contact me?

Has she already forgotten about me?

What's going to happen?

It's hard not knowing.

It pretty much sucks.

Bellmont is like a prison to me.

I'm here walking around, breathing, existing, but it feels like my life is somewhere else – someplace better.

Wherever Erin is.

I think about Erin every second of every day.

Erin.

Erin.

Erin.

Erin.

Erin.

Erin.

Erin.

Why hasn't she contacted me?

Why?

THIRTY-SEVEN

Later in the basketball season, Russ and I are sitting on my roof again, trying to look at stars, which is all we do anymore. He usually visits me after every game, although we never talk about b-ball. Sometimes we don't talk at all, but just look up at outer space. I've overheard my classmates talking trash about how well the team's doing. But I don't need to know anything more about it.

Russ says, 'Okay. Now I'm *really* worried about you.'

It's freezer-cold out, but I don't care. I enjoy the icy burn on my face and hands.

Russ is wrapped up in my comforter.

The sky is overcast, so there are no stars.

'Why?' I say, even though I know why. He's officially dropped the Boy21 charade for good, and has gone back to being Russ Allen, superstar basketball player. Since he's leading the conference in all categories, no one seems to mind that he was acting bonkers for most of the school year. Coach was right. Russ needed to play basketball more than I did. It's almost like I absorbed all of his craziness, like I was his leech, because he seems absolutely fine now, while I walk around school every day like I'm living on another planet.

'You've been angry and depressed. You seem to be getting worse.'

'So you're going to Duke?' I say, trying to change the subject.

There was an official press conference last week. News reporters came and videotaped Russ signing the agreement, accepting a scholarship. Everyone in the world knows he's going to Duke, so it was a stupid question to ask.

Russ nods. 'No word from Erin?'

'Nope.'

'Hasn't been that long.'

'It's been more than two months.'

'Already?'

The worst part is that no one else seems to notice Erin's not around. Her basketball team didn't win many games without her, and there were whispers at first, but the school keeps on going, as does everything else in Bellmont. It's like none of us really matter. Anyone could disappear and nothing would change too much. It's like our lives don't count.

'I hate Bellmont,' I say. 'I really hate it here.'

'Then leave. The world's a big place, Finley,' says Russ, sounding like Mr Gore for a moment. 'There are many good places in the world. I should know. I traveled around a lot, before I came here.'

'How am I going to leave?'

'Someday an opportunity will come. Think about Harry Potter. His life is terrible, but then a letter arrives, he gets on a train, and everything is different for him afterward. Better. Magical.'

'That's just a story.'

'So are we – we're stories too,' Russ says.

'What do you mean?'

'There're probably people who wouldn't think our lives are real either, if we wrote exactly what happened to us in a book.'

'I'm sorry I haven't come to watch you play ball. But I just can't.'

'No problem. Wes is a little pissed about your blowing off the book club, though.'

I shrug. I feel bad about blowing off Wes, but he hasn't exactly been friendly since Erin's accident. Everyone in school knows that the Irish mob moved Erin, and, because I'm the last remaining connection Erin has to Bellmont, people are afraid to be around me. Wes has been distant. I don't blame him.

'I'd like to take you somewhere once basketball season is over,' Russ says. 'Somewhere special.'

'Where?'

'It's a surprise.'

'Does it have anything to do with Erin?'

'No. It has to do with the cosmos. I think you'll like it.'

I'm surprised he brought up outer space, because it's been a while since he's mentioned *the cosmos*. 'Do you think that Erin will contact me?'

'Yeah, I do. *Eventually.*'

'Why hasn't she contacted me yet?'

'Don't know. We don't get to know why a lot in life. My therapist told me that.'

'Are you *better* now?'

Russ looks up at the gray sky.

'I mean, you don't call yourself Boy21 anymore,' I say. 'You don't talk about your parents flying around outer space in a rocket ship. You don't talk about leaving the planet. And you stopped wearing crazy costumes.'

'I wouldn't say I'm better. I'd say I don't need to hide right now.'

'Because things are going so well with basketball?'

'Because I'm moving on.'

'So it was all just a game. The outer-space stuff. You just made it up to keep people from asking you questions about what happened?'

'Sort of like you pretending that you don't talk?'

'That's not the same thing. I didn't lie to people. It was hard for me to talk – *too hard.*'

'Maybe so. And it was hard for me to be an Earthling too. You've been talking a lot more lately. More than you did when I met you, anyway. Does that mean you're better?'

I think about what he's implying, and maybe he's right. Maybe we were both playing roles just to get by.

'So what happened to your parents?' I ask.

'What happened to your mom?'

I'm not ready to talk about that, and it seems like Russ isn't either, because we sit on my roof silently for a long time before his grandfather pulls up in front of my home and Russ says, 'To be continued.'

I remain on the roof for a few more hours, and then I lie in bed looking up at the weird green glow of the galaxy Russ gave me.

THIRTY-EIGHT

The team loses the state championship game by one point. I hear Terrell missed the last shot. Russ – and everyone else – mourns the loss for a few weeks, students walking around the hallways with their heads down, teachers frowning, the entire school seeming depressed. But then life goes on and Russ remembers that he wants to show me something.

About a month or so after the big loss, on a Saturday, Russ and Mr Allen pick me up.

'You ready for your surprise?' Russ asks.

'Sure.'

I climb into the back of the Cadillac and watch Bellmont's ugliness slide across the window past my reflection.

Russ reads directions off a piece of paper and his grandfather makes the necessary turns.

After an hour or so of highway driving, we're on a

road with many trees, passing horses and cows even. I see cornstalks, fields of plants I can't identify, long stretches where there are no houses or streetlights or anything man-made at all.

I've never been to a place like this before, and it makes me sit up and swivel my head right and left so I don't miss anything.

The wind coming in through the window is warm and full of scents that seem so alive it almost hurts to breathe it all in.

'Manure,' Mr Allen says as we drive through an awful smell.

'What's that?' I say.

'Cow shit,' Russ says.

'Fertilizer,' Mr Allen says. 'Helps the crops grow.'

Even the manure smell is okay with me, because it's unlike anything I've experienced before – different than the smell of Bellmont's sewer system. To be clear, I don't like the manure smell, but I like being in the countryside.

We take a bumpy dirt road through the woods and I get a little nervous, because if we break down out here, there's nothing around for miles.

But then I spot what looks like a gas station. A sign outside reads STAR WATCHER'S PARADISE! There's actually an exclamation point, which makes this place seem extra exciting. We pull up to the gas pump. Mr Allen fills the tank and I follow Russ inside, where there's a worn wooden floor and a few aisles of food and camping supplies. A large red-faced man sits behind the counter.

'Howdy,' he says, and shows us his pink palm.

'We have a reservation,' Russ says. 'It's under Allen.'

'Sure thing! You picked a beautiful night. No clouds at all. Your eyes are in for a feast!'

'We've been checking the weather all week,' Russ says.

'How's viewing station number twelve sound?'

'Fine,' Russ says.

Mr Allen enters the store and stands next to us.

The man writes something down on a piece of paper and then hands us each a brochure. 'These are our viewing rules. Unless it's an emergency, do not turn your car on until first light. You must pull the blackout shades in your station if you have a light on inside. Absolutely no flashlights or lights of any kind may be used outside of your station. Once the sun goes down, library voices are mandatory, which means you need to whisper. You'll be asked to leave if you hoot and holler. Other than that, just enjoy the show. I'll need you each to sign the rules brochure to verify that you agree to the terms.'

Mr Allen gives the man a credit card. We all sign the papers, receive complimentary star charts, and then get back into the car.

'What *is* this place?' I say. 'What's the show?'

'You'll see,' Russ answers.

We drive down the dirt road and pass numbered wooden signs marking unpaved driveways that bend and disappear into the woods.

When we find number twelve, Mr Allen makes a left and we drive on a dirt road so narrow, branches whack the car. 'I better not see any scratches on my Cadillac, or someone named Russ is going to be waxing and buffing all day tomorrow,' says Mr Allen.

The road curves off to the right and then we come upon a strange-looking structure that sort of looks like a cross between a tree house and a lighthouse. It's an eight-sided tower that rises up and out of the woods. A huge bucket sits on top. The building reminds me of that piece in chess that looks like a castle.

'Well, I'll be,' Mr Allen says, but he's smiling.

'Come on,' Russ says.

We enter through a door on the ground and then climb a spiral staircase to the center of a room with four beds and two windows that have heavy curtains – the blackout shades, I assume. There's a small bathroom too. Just a sink and a toilet – no shower.

Russ keeps climbing and I follow until we have to push up what looks like a trapdoor in the ceiling. It opens to the sky and we climb onto a viewing deck that has a tall wooden railing, so that it seems like we're standing in a gigantic wooden cup. The floor is covered with what feels like a wrestling mat. My feet sink an inch or so into it.

'This is where we'll sleep tonight,' Russ says. 'The beds inside are for the old man.'

I look around and see nothing but new green leaves of early spring trees and the tops of the dozen or so other viewing towers, which are spaced maybe one hundred yards apart and form a circle.

'This is amazing,' I say.

'What have I been telling you?' Russ says. 'There's more to the world than Bellmont, right?'

We race down the steps and carry the cooler and other supplies up into the sleeping room.

It takes Mr Allen a long time to climb the steps, but when he reaches the top, he looks around and says, 'I've never seen so many trees.'

'Who knew that you could drive two hours and be somewhere like this?' I say.

Russ smiles proudly.

We eat the tuna fish sandwiches Mrs Allen packed for us and drink root beer as the sunset shoots fire across the treetops.

'I don't want to be climbing steps in the dark, so I'm going to settle in downstairs with my book. You two have fun, and don't get too close to the edge, you hear?' Mr Allen says, and then he disappears into the hatch.

It's getting cooler up here; there's a stiff breeze and the trees are making a lot of noise.

'Do you hear the leaves hissing?' I say.

'Cool, huh? Almost time for "library voices,"' Russ says, making air quotes. 'I bet sound really carries up here.'

We both lie down on our backs and my shoulder blades sink into the mat.

'This place is truly awesome,' I say. 'Thanks for bringing me.'

He nods and then we watch the western sky glow an orange-pink.

We lie there in silence for fifteen minutes or so, and then, out of nowhere, Russ says, 'Tell me what happened to your mother and I'll tell you what happened to my parents.'

'Why?'

'Because that's what friends do – they talk to each other and listen.'

'It doesn't matter.'

'It does.'

'I'm not supposed to talk about it.'

'Don't you trust me?' Russ asks.

'I do.'

'Well, then. Just me and trees around.'

'Is that why you brought me out here?'

'It's part of the reason. And I'd prefer to talk before the show begins.'

'The stars?'

'Yeah.'

'We look at stars on my roof all the time.'

'This is different. You'll see,' he says. 'Let's talk about what happened to our parents. I really think it might help. I talk to my therapist all the time. You should probably be talking to a therapist too.'

'I've been talking to Mr Gore.'

'That's good. Talk to me.'

'It's a depressing story.'

'So's mine.'

'I don't know.'

'We'll use library voices, so it won't really count anyway.'

I smile. *Library voices*. I want to know Russ's story, and I don't really care anymore about keeping Pop's secrets, especially since Erin's gone missing. Maybe that's why the bad stuff happens in neighborhoods like mine, because no one talks. But even so, I'm surprised when I hear myself using the library voice – when I hear myself telling the story for the first time.

I tell Russ about how my grandfather stole money from the thugs he worked for so he could take my grandmother back to Ireland. She had terminal cancer and wanted to die in her homeland. They were born in County Cork – we still have family there – but they were always too poor to make the trip back. I've never been to Ireland, but returning before she died was very important to my grandmother. So, out of desperation and grief, Pop stole the money and took her, thinking they'd be safe once they were out of America. The only problem – the rest of his family was still in Bellmont. My pop underestimated the ruthlessness of his coworkers. The thugs Pop worked for took me to get to my grandfather – to get him to come back from Ireland.

'What do you mean they *took you*?' Russ says, using his library voice.

I allow myself to remember. Remembering makes me feel like someone's jabbing a finger into my throat. I begin to feel sweaty.

'My grandfather was mixed up with bad men – men like Erin's brother, Rod. Probably hard for you to imagine.'

'So they *kidnapped* you?'

I swallow. 'I haven't talked about this with anyone – not even Erin.'

'It's good to talk. You can trust me.'

I search the sky above for early stars, see none, and then tell him what I remember.

I remember men in ski masks taking me in the middle of the night, my parents screaming, and the sound of my father being beaten.

I remember being thrown into a car trunk – my hands tied behind my back, an awful sock in my mouth, tape around my head.

I remember being in a dark room for a long time, peeing in my pants because I was so scared, smelling only dried urine and dust for what seemed like weeks, being hungry and thirsty, and then suddenly I was with my father again, only it was at my mother's funeral and my pop no longer had legs.

I remember my father's eyes were so red – like raw-hamburger red – and his face was still bruised purple and yellow. I remember Dad telling me that my mother went to the police and tried to rescue me, but that was why she was dead, and then he told me that I could never tell anyone about what happened – ever. I was never allowed to tell a single person, or else we *all* might end up dead.

'He told me not to snitch, and so I didn't. I was just a little kid. And I was so afraid of saying the wrong thing – losing my dad and pop too.'

'So that's when you stopped talking?' Russ says.

'Yeah. It's also when I started playing basketball.'

'Damn.'

'I can't remember what my mother looks like,' I say. 'We have photos, but I can't see her anymore outside of the picture frames. Do you know what I mean?'

'Sometimes I feel like I'm forgetting the sound of my father's voice,' Russ says. 'What my mother smelled like. So many things.'

'What happened to them?'

It's like the western trees are lined with pink neon now. This is the last of today's light.

Russ takes a deep breath, and then says, 'Carjacking.

Mom and Dad went to see a friend play saxophone at a bar in a shady neighborhood. Some crackheads shot both my parents in the head and then ran off with a few hundred bucks, my mom's jewelry, and my dad's watch. Completely random act of violence. Completely unfair. Stupid. Enough to make you want to check out for a while and tell people you're from outer space.'

'What do you see,' I ask, not really sure *why* I'm asking, 'when you try to remember your parents together? What's your best memory?'

He thinks for a few minutes. 'This one time I went to see my father play with a throwback old-time-style big band, and halfway through the set the leader asked my mom to join him onstage to sing a song. I was surprised because I didn't even know my mom could sing.

'She didn't want to get up, but the audience started to clap for her, so she took the stage and said, "You boys know my song." My father switched to trumpet, because he could play any instrument. He played the opening notes, and then my mother sang Ella Fitzgerald's "I'm Beginning to See the Light." My father stood next to her and they sort of communicated with music.

'Mom was singing. Dad was playing trumpet. But their eyes were locked the whole time and I could tell they were so in love. The crowd clapped for five minutes straight when they finished, which embarrassed my mom. I could tell because she kept shaking her head and wouldn't make eye contact with anyone.

'"You sing?" I remember asking her when she sat down next to me. And she said, "I used to, a long time ago."'

'As we watched the rest of the show, I remember wondering how many other things I didn't know about my parents. You only get to know so much.'

When it's clear that Russ is done talking, I say, 'That's a beautiful memory.'

'Do you have one like that of your parents together?'

I think hard for a minute. 'No. Not like that one.'

Russ doesn't say anything in response, so I worry that he feels bad about sharing his good memory when I don't have one to match his. I don't want him to feel bad, so I say, 'But someday, I might tell someone about stargazing with the NBA's best point guard, Russ Allen, back before he was famous.'

'Let's not talk about basketball, okay?' Russ doesn't say anything else, which makes me think that it was really hard for him to talk about his parents.

The sky goes from navy to black. And then all of a sudden millions of stars blink above us, and Russ whispers, 'I think the show has begun.'

It's almost like someone flicked a switch, because there were only a few stars here and there, and now there's an endless supply – like a huge diamond exploded in the sky.

'It's so beautiful,' I say, because I've never seen anything like it before.

'Whenever I think the world is ugly – that life has no meaning at all – I remind myself that this is here, always waiting for me,' Russ says. 'I can always look up at the cosmos and marvel, no matter what happens. And when I look up at it, I feel as though my problems are small. I don't know why, but it always makes me feel better.'

'And that's enough?' I ask. 'Just looking at stars?'

'It can be,' Russ says.

I expect Russ to begin naming all the constellations, but he doesn't.

We lie silently under outer space, taking in all those pinpricks of light, and I too feel dwarfed by the massive universe.

I wonder if Erin is also looking up at stars tonight, maybe sitting on some roof somewhere, thinking about me.

I wonder if my mom's up there in heaven or simply up there *somewhere* – maybe even on some after-death spaceship or something, like Boy21 had imagined.

'Why do you think we met?' I ask. 'Do you think I was supposed to help you return to basketball? Was it fate?'

'It's because my parents were murdered by crackheads,' he says. 'I'd be in L.A. if my parents were still alive. Other than that, I don't know.'

'But you're here somehow,' I whisper.

'And so are you,' Russ whispers back.

We lie next to each other in silence all night, looking up at the impossible mind-blowing awesomeness of the universe, and I don't think either of us sleeps a minute.

THIRTY-NINE

On the anniversary of my mother's murder, just like every other year, Dad, Pop, and I lay flowers on her grave – Cathy McManus.

June sun.

Blue skies.

No one else is in the graveyard.

Standing there, gazing at the endless rows of headstones, it feels like we're the only three people left in the world.

As far as my eyes can see, white and gray grave markers line the earth, each with a tiny bit of information. Name, years lived, maybe a nice quote. But not enough to really let you know who these people were. I wonder if each marker has a story just as complicated as my mom's.

Like every other year, I remember the kidnapping, think about the courage it took for my mother to go to the police, and wish I'd gotten the chance to know her better.

In his wheelchair, in front of the grave, Pop talks to my mom and says he's sorry over and over again, cries a lot, and is a guilty mess.

'When you get your chance to leave Bellmont,' Dad says to me, 'take it.'

His face is tense. Wrinkles shoot out from the corners of his eyes. He's staring at Pop in this really weird way. It's like he loves and hates the old man simultaneously.

'You hear me?' Dad asks.

'Yeah.'

When I was little, I used to think that we visited my mom's grave because she was somehow there – like we were really going to spend time with her ghost or something like that. Now I realize we go so Pop can repent.

I wonder about my mom.

This might sound dumb, but the only thing I really remember was that she loved green Life Savers, which she called the Irish Life Savers. She used to buy a roll almost every day and feed me as many as it took to get to the first green one, which she'd eat.

This was our little ritual.

We'd walk to the corner store in search of her daily green Irish Life Saver.

It's a stupid thing to remember, but it's what I have. And the truth is, I've always gotten very nervous whenever I see someone eating Life Savers, or if I see a roll in the store. I worry that if I look too closely I'll discover that green Life Savers don't exist. I'm terrified of maybe realizing that I made up the only detail about my mom I own, and then I'll have absolutely nothing left.

Maybe that's a dumb thing to worry about, but it's just who I am – what life has given me.

Dad never talks about Mom anymore – ever.

And Dad never eats Life Savers either – at least I've never seen him eat one.

When we leave the cemetery, Dad spends the rest of the day with Pop. I spend it alone on the roof, hoping that Erin will crawl through my bedroom window and snuggle up to me, like she did so many times before. But Erin doesn't show up.

FORTY

The morning before my high-school graduation cere-
mony, while we're eating our eggs and bacon in the
kitchen, Pop hands me a plain white envelope.

'What's this?'

'Open it,' Dad says.

I tear it open and pull out the contents. There's some
sort of ticket that reads AMTRAK.

'Amtrak?' I ask.

'It's a train. You do know what trains are, right?' Pop
asks.

'Why are you giving me a train ticket?'

'Graduation present,' Dad says.

'To where?'

'Read the ticket,' Pop says.

'New Hampshire? Why did you buy me a ticket to
New Hampshire?'

'We didn't buy it,' Pop says.

'Read the letter,' Dad says.

I unfold the paper and immediately recognize Erin's handwriting. My heart nearly explodes and I start to sweat. *Erin!* I stand and walk into the living room.

'Where you going?' Pop says, and I can hear laughter in his voice.

Finley,

You don't know how much I've missed you. You can't imagine how much I wanted to contact you in the past six months. It's been torture. I hope you don't think I didn't want to see you back at the hospital. I didn't have a choice. I wasn't calling the shots, which I'm sure you've figured out by now.

I can't say much in this letter. I'm not allowed.

I'm somewhere very unlike Bellmont. It's beautiful. People are nice to each other. You can walk the streets alone at night. Everything is so clean! You could eat off the sidewalk. So many stars! Trees everywhere! I have my own tiny apartment, if you can believe that. And I'm already enrolled at a small liberal arts college and set to begin this fall, although I won't be playing basketball. Things have been taken care of. That's all I can say in this letter. Oh, and I'm going by Katie Reidy now. Do you like the name? Can you get used to it?

Do you want to come live with me?

I'm serious. Seems like your family still has some friends left because it's been taken care of, as they say.

You can't tell anyone where you're going and you'll have to change your name. I'm thinking we'll call you Lucas Williams. How about that? Do you like it? It has a nice ring, doesn't it?

I have enough money for us to live a decent life. You could apply to the college and who knows? Or you can get a job.

I'll explain everything if you come. I hope you will come. I love you. Please get on the train. Just come. Trust me. Please.

Love,
The Girlfriend Formerly Known As Erin

I run back into the kitchen and say, 'What is this? Is this for real?'

'It's a chance to get out of here and start fresh,' Dad says. 'Free and clear of your family history. It's a chance at life.'

'Where did this note come from?' I ask.

'Don't ask questions,' Pop says. 'This is the real deal. A true chance. No strings attached.'

'How do we know it's not a trap?'

'A trap? You've been watching too many movies,' Pop says. 'If they wanted to hurt you, they'd come to the house and hurt you. They wouldn't buy you a train ticket and hurt you in New Hampshire.'

'What did you have to do to make this happen?' I ask.

'Nothing,' Dad says. 'Except promise silence.'

'I'm not stupid,' I say.

Dad and Pop look at each other.

'Let's just say,' Pop says, 'some of the older guys still feel bad about what happened to you when you were a kid, but they respected the fact that we kept our mouths shut when the cops came asking questions all those years ago. There are rules, but we're not all monsters. Most guys do what they can when they can.'

'The train leaves in two hours, so you have to make your decision now,' Dad says. 'If you go, you can't come back to Bellmont. Ever. And you'll have to be careful about contacting us. They'll explain the rules to you and you'll have no choice but to obey every one.'

'Why?'

'Those are the terms. We don't get to ask why.'

I remember what Russ said about not being able to know why.

I sit at the table opposite Pop and Dad and notice that their physical similarities are striking. I wonder if they're thinking I look like a younger version of them. Three generations of McManuses.

'So I'm going away on mob money?' I say quietly.

'You're going away,' Pop says. 'You're not going to be taken care of for life. You're just getting a ticket out of here and a chance to start over someplace better.'

I think about it and wonder about ethics. Do I really

want to accept mob money, even if it's only a little to help me relocate? Could I live with myself? After all they've done to my family, am I owed this?

'And if I don't go?' I say.

Dad shrugs. 'Then you go to community college and live in Bellmont for another two years, minimum. And maybe you lose your best friend forever. This is most likely a one-shot chance here.'

'Will Rod be up there? Mr and Mrs Quinn?'

'Don't know,' Pop says.

I absolutely want to see Erin. But I don't know about the rest. How can I choose between the two men who raised me – the only family I have – and the girl who's been at my side since elementary school? It's easy to choose between Bellmont and anywhere else, because I don't want to end up alone rotting away in a row home drinking myself to death. I definitely want out of this town, but I don't want to leave Pop and Dad behind.

'What do you think I should do?'

They look at their hands. Their eyes are welling up. They've already decided what I should do, which is why they gave me the envelope. But the final choice is mine alone.

The doorbell rings.

'That's Russ,' I say.

'Don't tell him anything,' Dad says.

I cross the living room, pinching myself to make sure I'm not dreaming.

When I open the door, Russ peers through the screen and says, 'What's up?'

'I'm not going to school today,' I say. 'Not gonna walk in graduation.'

'Why not? You sick?'

I don't want to lie to Russ, especially since I know this might be the last time I ever speak with him.

'What's going on, man?' he says. 'You all right?'

I think about what I can say to make him understand, and when I have it, I smile. 'I just got a ticket to Hogwarts.'

'What?'

'Might be taking a train ride to a magical place that's much better than here. Don't tell any Muggles, okay? But I want you to know I'll be all right.'

Russ squints through the screen for a moment before he returns my smile and says, 'She finally contacted you.'

'I can neither confirm nor deny that statement.'

'I have no idea what's going on, but I feel like I should hug you.'

'We can do that.' I step outside the house.

Russ and I hug. A real hug. Four arms. Big squeeze to say all the things we can't or maybe won't.

'I'm not going to ever see you again, am I?' Russ says.

'Dunno.'

'Be good to yourself, Finley. I wish you a beautiful life.'

'I wish you a beautiful life too – many clear starry nights, and a few collegiate basketball records,' I say.

Russ looks into my eyes the way he did when he first came to Bellmont – like he's communicating with me – then smiles sadly and walks away.

I watch him stride down the street and he throws a few sky punches, which I take as a sign of approval, like he's happy for me, so I return to the kitchen.

'You going to get on the train?' Dad says.

I'm scared to leave my family. It's hard for me to think of being anywhere but Bellmont. Then I remember the night I spent with Russ in the country, how there are other places in the world, better places, and I say, 'I'd really like to see Erin.'

Pop nods once and then looks out the window. I'm surprised when he closes his eyes, fingers Grandmom's rosary beads, and starts to mouth words. I've never seen Pop pray before.

Dad and I go upstairs and pack up my belongings, which aren't much. I stuff clothes and jackets and shoes into a duffel bag. Peel a few stars off the ceiling and slip those in too. I grab my framed picture of Mom and Dad and me, from back in the day, and then I find my basketball in the garage, because maybe Erin will want to shoot around.

Pop and Dad drive me to Thirtieth Street Station in Philadelphia, and on the way there they explain that a man will meet me in New Hampshire and that I am to ask no questions – none whatsoever. He will drive me to Erin, but he won't say anything to me at all. I'll know who he is, because he'll call me Lucas.

'This seems crazy,' I say. 'I'm a little freaked out.'

'You'll be fine,' Dad says.

'You've already been through the worst part of your life,' Pop says. 'Go be with Erin. She's a good woman who loves you – the key to your happiness. Trust me. I know, because your grandmother was an even better woman. I would do anything to be with her now. *Anything.*'

We park outside of a huge white building. Cars, taxis, and people are everywhere.

'Finley,' Pop says, just before I get out of the car. I turn around and am surprised to see the old man trembling. 'I'm sorry.'

'It's okay, Pop.'

'Your grandmother would have wanted you to have this.' Pop pulls her rosary beads over his head and then extends his arm toward me so that the black crucifix is dangling right in front of my face. 'Maybe it will bring you luck.'

'I can't take that.' I don't even know what the rosary means, which prayers go with which beads, and they've been around Pop's neck or fist ever since my grandmother died.

'You *will* take it, Finley. Put it around your neck, under your shirt. If you only wear it one day in your life, let it be today. And then pass it down to your children when the time comes.'

I put the necklace on and open the back car door to give Pop a hug. His cheek is wet when it brushes against mine.

Dad carries my bag and basketball. I follow him into the building, through what seems to be a food court, and into a beautiful room with a high ceiling and great columns. It reminds me a little of the Franklin Institute, where I saw that IMAX movie about stars and repairing the Hubble Space Telescope. I remember how Boy21 freaked out and left when he saw the space shuttle. How I wanted to follow him but wasn't allowed.

Dad and I check the departure times on a board that changes by flipping numbers and making this ticking noise.

'That's your train,' Dad says, pointing.

We walk to the right staircase and I get in line with my ticket and Erin's letter in my hand.

'I really feel like I'm going to Hogwarts,' I say.

'What's Hogwarts?'

'Never mind.' I suddenly wish I'd told Dad about Harry Potter, but this isn't the time. Maybe I'll send him a copy in the mail.

'I'm sorry I wasn't able to give you a better childhood, Finley.'

Dad's eyelids are trembling now too, and in front of all these strangers. I really hope he doesn't cry. I won't be able to get on the train if he cries.

'Dad,' I say, but nothing else comes.

'Whenever you get to missing us – if you do—'

'I will definitely—'

'Think about your old man collecting tolls at three in the morning and your legless pop drinking beer all day, wearing a diaper. Go get yourself a better life. Do whatever it takes to make a good life for you and Erin. Irish people have been leaving their homes in search of better lives for many, many years. We're very good at it. So go make the Irish proud.'

I hug Dad and start to feel the finality of what's happening. I start to feel the tears coming.

But then the line starts moving and it's time to board.

'Erin will let you know the best way to contact us, but don't *worry* about us, okay?' Dad says. 'Be a good man.'

'Love you, Dad.'

'We love you too.' Dad sticks his hand in my pocket, but before I can check to see what he put in there he's handing me my bag and basketball, the ticket man is asking to see my ticket, and then I'm halfway down the stairs, looking over my shoulder at Dad, who is crying now and waving good-bye from above.

The platform is full of hot sticky air, and I'm surprised that my train is air-conditioned.

After seeing other people do it, I shove my bag into the space above my seat, and then sit down.

My heart's pounding.

I've never been on a train before.

I wonder if I'll meet friends during the ride, like Harry Potter did. I start to look around, but all I see are tired and grumpy-looking adults.

I settle into the seat, reread Erin's letter, and try to feel hopeful for the future. I wonder if New Hampshire is as beautiful as the Star Watcher's Paradise. Erin was and is beautiful enough to make even Bellmont tolerable, so I close my eyes and imagine her face.

The train lurches forward and we pull out of Thirtieth Street Station.

A woman wearing a special train hat comes and inspects my ticket, which is sort of fun.

I watch Philadelphia and then so many towns I can't name pass by my reflection in the window.

So much had to happen to land me on this train – thinking about that makes it feel like someone's kicking in my skull, and then, suddenly, I'm thinking about the unfathomable stars Russ and I saw from the viewing station in the woods. We really don't get to understand *why* most of the time. It's true.

I reach into my pocket and pull out five one-hundred-dollar bills, which is more money than I have ever held in my hand, and may very well be Dad's life savings. I think about Dad and Pop living alone without me. Who will help Pop in the bathroom and put him to bed? *Why didn't I think about that before?* They loved having Erin and me around. The house will be so quiet now. Pop will probably drink even more. I start to feel guilty about leaving, like I might even cry. I grasp a handful of shirt and the four points of my grandmother's crucifix dig into my palm.

'Where you going?' the woman across the aisle says. She's a big lady wearing a purple dress and a little hat that matches.

'New Hampshire,' I say, before I remember that I'm not supposed to tell anyone my destination.

'Pretty country up there.'

'Hope so.'

'First time?'

'Yes, ma'am.'

'You going to play basketball?' she says, eyeing my ball on the seat next to me.

'I hope so – with my girlfriend.'

'You sure do hope a lot.'

I smile at her.

'Nothing wrong with hoping,' she says, and then looks out her window.

Suddenly, the reality of what's happened hits me. Everything's swirling in my chest. I'm so nervous. I already miss Pop and Dad. It's hard to wrap my mind around this moment. Life can change so quickly. Maybe this is how Russ felt when he first came to Bellmont? No wonder he invented Boy21.

I don't want to cry on the train, so I close my eyes and visualize playing basketball against Erin, and we're little kids again in my backyard, silently shooting on the old adjustable rim.

It's a good image, but I force my mind to see the future, what will happen when I arrive in New Hampshire.

It takes some imagining, but finally I see myself playing H.O.R.S.E. with Erin as the sun sets through the trees and the stars poke through the endless sky above. I see us holding hands, getting older through the years, even raising kids in a nice neighborhood where they won't have to worry about the things we had to worry about. And then Erin and I are kissing on a new roof, under the same endless unknowable space above, and somehow we're okay.

ACKNOWLEDGMENTS

Many, many people have helped and inspired me along the way, and I thank all of them. The following – in one way or another – are responsible for *Boy21* ending up in your hands: Doug Stewart and everyone at Sterling Lord Literistic; Alvina Ling, Connie Hsu, Bethany Strout, Emma Ledbetter, Ames O'Neill, and everyone at Little, Brown; Megan, Micah and Kelly, Mom and Dad, Barb and Peague, Uncle Pete, Big H and Dink; Roland Merullo; Evan James Roskos; Mark Wiltsey; Dr Len Altamura and Kate Cranston; Bill and Mo Rhoda; Tim and Beth Rayworth; Jean Wertz; Wally Wilhoit; Canadian Scott Caldwell; Peruvian Scott Humfeld; Heather Leah; Liz Jensen; Sara Zarr; Dave Tavani; Kent Green and Ernie Rockelman (aka Emerald Productions); Lars and Drea (LA Auto!); Scott Warnock; Drew Giorgi; and, most of all, my wife / therapist / first reader / editor / cheerleader / love of my life / muse / best friend, Alicia Bessette (aka Al).